'If you could **where on my** **kiss land?'**

This was sheer torture, Matt thought, forcing his gaze to remain on hers. 'Your stomach.'

'Really? Why?'

'Because I'm intrigued by the miracle within you.'

Tears gathered in her eyes at his words. It was possibly the nicest thing anyone had ever said to her.

PRACTISING AND PREGNANT

Dedicated doctors, determinedly single— and unexpectedly pregnant

These dedicated doctors have one goal in life—to heal patients and save lives. They've little time for love, but somehow it finds them. When they're faced with single parenthood too, how do they juggle the demands and dilemmas of their professional and private lives?

PRACTISING AND PREGNANT

Emotionally entangled stories of doctors in love from Mills & Boon® Medical Romance™.

THE DOCTOR'S GIFT

BY
LUCY CLARK

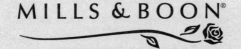

MILLS & BOON®

To my mum—Glenda.
Thanks for being there whenever I've needed you.
You're a shining example of motherhood.

Pr 23:25

First published in Great Britain 2003
Harlequin Mills & Boon Limited,
Eton House, 18-24 Paradise Road, Richmond, Surrey TW9 1SR

© Lucy Clark 2003

ISBN 0 263 83433 6

Set in Times Roman 10½ on 11½ pt.
03-0303-51489

Printed and bound in Spain
by Litografia Rosés, S.A., Barcelona

CHAPTER ONE

'WHAT'S that noise?' Rhea asked, walking from their medical clinic to the footpath. The loud roaring noise reverberated down the street.

Matt locked the door behind him and followed his sister. 'That, Rhea, is the sound of a motorbike—a Harley by the sound of it.' They waited a few more seconds before the object making the noise came into view.

'How did you know that? You don't even like motorbikes.'

Matt shrugged. 'I'm a guy.' He looked at the rider, dressed in black leather, and realised the form was feminine. *Very* feminine. The bike slowed down to a crawl before stopping in front of them. The rider stretched out her foot and placed it on the ground. The black leathers hugged her curves like the bike probably hugged the road.

Kelly looked at the man before her. So *this* was Matthew Bentley. She'd recognised Rhea, of course, as the two women had met at the interview, but Matthew had been at a medical conference. Even so, with both of them standing outside an old converted house with a sign that stated it was the Bright Family Practice, black medical bags at their feet, she still would have known she'd found the right people.

Taking the opportunity to study Matt more closely from beneath her helmet visor, Kelly felt butterflies start to spin around in her stomach. He was *gorgeous*. His short dark hair was neat and tidy and his brow was puckered into a frown. His blue eyes were watching her closely and his lips were in a grim line. Kelly knew instinctively that his entire face would light up if he curved those lips into a true smile.

And he was tall! She liked them tall. A lovely six feet three inches, she was positive.

She slid her visor up and met his gaze. 'Wanna ride?' She was surprised at how husky and intimate her tone sounded. She'd only meant to tease him because he was scowling at her, yet from the way his eyebrows raised momentarily, she realised he'd interpreted her words in a completely different way.

The scowl was back a second later. 'No—thank you.'

'Kelly!' Rhea smiled warmly. 'Glad you could make it.'

'*You're* Dr O'Shea,' Matt stated.

Kelly kept her gaze on him as she pulled off her gloves, undid the strap beneath her chin and slowly pulled her helmet off. She closed her eyes and shook her red curls free.

Matt felt his gut tighten at the sight of those beautiful red locks spilling around her shoulders. He'd had no idea the new doctor was a redhead! He had a weakness for redheads, especially ones with vivid green eyes—just like Kelly's. He swallowed over the attraction, pushing it from his mind.

'Sure am.' She rested her helmet on one leather-clad thigh and held out a hand to him. 'I take it you're Matt.'

He politely shook her hand, forcing himself to ignore the warmth that filled him at her touch. He must be imagining things. Matt dropped her hand as though burnt. 'We were expecting you yesterday afternoon. You're twenty-four hours late.'

Kelly was a little taken back by his attitude. 'I understood I was starting work this evening.' She glanced at Rhea. 'Did I get it wrong?'

'No, but we were beginning to worry.'

'Oh, I'm sorry,' she replied earnestly. 'I had car trouble.'

'So I see,' Matt commented, eyeing the bike distastefully.

'You don't like bikes?'

'Pushbikes are fine,' he retorted. 'I'm late. I'll see you at the hospital tonight.' With that, he picked up his medical bag and walked across the bitumen.

'Don't mind him,' Rhea said. 'Let's get you settled in. It's just over here.' She pointed to the house across the street. Kelly looked towards where she was pointing but instead watched as Matt strode purposefully away, his back ramrod straight, and into the house next door. 'Matt lives to the left of you and my house is to the right.'

'And your parents are in the middle. How cosy.' Kelly smiled at the tall brunette. When she'd come to Bright for her interview four weeks ago, she'd instantly liked Rhea Dawson. Matt's father had been there as well and it was his position Kelly was filling for six months. Part of the package was living in their house, which suited her fine.

'Did my boxes arrive?'

'Yes. They came yesterday. Matt said he put them inside.'

'Great.' Kelly brought the bike back to life and shifted forward. 'Do *you* want a ride?'

'I thought you'd never ask.' Rhea giggled.

'Patient's name is William Davidson. Thirty-two-year-old lawyer visiting from Melbourne. He's staying with friends here in Bright and they found him unconscious in their spare room.' Matt continued with the briefing. 'I saw Mr Davidson in my clinic yesterday when he presented with flu symptoms. Runny nose, puffy eyes. I didn't prescribe anti-biotics as it was a viral infection that will clear up in a few days if Mr Davidson keeps warm.'

He looked at Kelly. 'Dr O'Shea, as it's your first night here, it might be better if you assist me even though you have a very impressive résumeé regarding Accident and Emergency procedures.'

'Certainly, but I think it might be easier if you call me Kelly. It's a little less formal, especially when you need a retractor or something like that.' She smiled at him but he merely nodded.

She was leaning up against the wall in A and E, dressed, like the rest of them, in green theatre scrubs. She'd somehow managed to tame her curls into a bun which sat right on top of her head, and it made her look taller—even though he guessed her to be about five feet nine. He looked away, making himself concentrate on finishing the briefing.

'I don't have any more details on the patient so I have no idea what we're going to find when he arrives. I'd like a chest X-ray taken, to make sure there are no complications arising in his lungs.'

'Does he suffer from asthma?' Kelly asked, trying to push away the spark of attraction which shot through her every time she looked into her colleague's deep blue eyes.

'No. He wasn't currently taking any medication except for paracetamol. He actually became quite annoyed when I refused to prescribe the antibiotics, but his symptoms simply didn't warrant it.'

'No cold or flu tablets? Nothing like that?'

'Not that he mentioned, just paracetamol.'

'OK.' Kelly nodded. 'Anything else?'

'Not at this stage.'

'I guess we'll find out more soon. If that's all, I think I'll visit the little girls' room before he arrives.' With that, she hurried from the room.

Matt headed to the treatment room and checked over instruments they might need. He breathed in, smelling an exotic spicy scent which lingered in the room. Kelly. She'd been in here just before their briefing and although her perfume wasn't strong or overpowering it was subtly winding its way around the thirty-three-bed hospital.

Physically, he couldn't deny she was gorgeous. There was no disputing that fact, but she was also dangerous. He'd dated women like her in the past. Women who flitted through life without a care in the world where the only thing they'd give him was a very bad headache and a broken heart. Well, regardless of how incredibly sexy he found Dr O'Shea—Kelly, he mentally corrected—he was determined to hold himself aloof. She was a colleague. That was all, *and* she was only here for six months.

'Ambulance is pulling in,' one of the nursing staff announced.

Matt was about to call for Kelly but she walked into the room and quickly scrubbed, pulling on a protective gown and gloves. Mr Davidson was brought in and transferred to the hospital barouche.

'Obs, and get an IV in, stat,' Matt ordered.

Kelly reached for a medical torch and checked the patient's pupils while the nurses continued to remove Mr Davidson's clothing. 'Pupils are dilated.' Kelly frowned as she pressed two fingers to the man's carotid pulse. 'What's his BP?'

'Eight over fifty,' one of the nurses announced.

'Take a look at his eyes, Matt.' Kelly handed the torch over. 'Breathing is shallow. Check him for—'

'*What?*' The patient erupted, sitting bolt upright on the hospital bed, knocking the medical torch flying from Matt's hand, his other arm connecting across Kelly's chest and shoulder. The force was so strong that she actually lost her balance and fell down. 'What do you think you're doing?' he demanded, glaring at the people around him.

'Kelly?' There was an urgent note in Matt's tone.

'I'm all right. Just a little shaken,' she replied, as one of the nurses helped her to her feet.

'What do you think you're doing?' Mr Davidson demanded again.

Kelly ripped off her gloves and tugged on another pair as one of the nurses changed her protective gown. She watched Mr Davidson closely. 'Mr Davidson, you passed out. Your friends were worried.'

'I'm fine,' he shouted. One of the nurses took a step towards him and he turned quickly, his movements jerky. 'Stay away from me. Stay away.' He noticed the IV line in his arm and ripped it from his body as though he didn't have a care in the world.

'Mr Davidson…' Matt said quietly, and their patient swung around to look at him.

'I said stay away.' His arm was bleeding where the IV had been, but it didn't seem to bother him. Kelly watched as he started scratching his arms and then legs with intensity. 'Bugs! Look what you've done to me. I've got bugs all over me. Get them off! Get them off! They're going to get me. They're getting into me!' He was shouting at the top of his lungs, hysteria mounting within him.

'All right, we'll get them off,' Matt soothed. 'Just let me take a closer look.'

Mr Davidson gripped his head in pain and seconds later passed out again. The instant he was down, Matt and Kelly rushed forward.

'Check his arms,' she ordered. 'And his ankles.' Matt was listening to Mr Davidson's chest and Kelly flicked the torchlight into his eyes. 'Pupils are huge.'

'Get that IV line back in and get that blood cleaned up,' Matt demanded.

'When you saw him did he also complain of headaches? Migraine-like headaches?'

'Yes.'

'Sore mouth?'

'Yes.'

Kelly nodded. 'He's coked out.'

'Coked out?' one of the nurses asked. 'Does that mean a drug overdose?'

'Yes,' Kelly replied.

'But what is he coked out on?' Matt asked rhetorically.

'Fresh needle mark in the left ankle,' the nurse stated.

'Right, everyone take level-one protective measures.' Matt was firmly in command. 'Double gloves and gowns. Take a blood sample to test for HIV. Anyone with scratches, get them properly covered up. You know the protocol. Get those ECG lines on him, stat.'

Kelly waited for Matt to return before she did the same. 'My guess is cocaine. Formication is a dead give-away of toxic psychosis. Anticipate intubation and defibrillation.'

'I'm sorry, did you say fornication?' the anaesthetist asked incredulously as he set up the ECG leads so they could monitor Mr Davidson's heart rate more closely.

'No. *Formication*—the word has an *m*, not an *n*. It's where the patient thinks bugs or ants are crawling under their skin.'

'Interesting,' the anaesthetist replied.

'The slightest twinge on that ECG and I want to know,' Matt instructed. 'Is the Narcan ready?'

'Uh, don't give him Narcan,' Kelly interjected quickly. 'Better to give him Haldol—haloperidol. It's an antipsychotic drug—and also Valium to relax him.'

'Do we *have* any haloperidol?' Matt fired at a nurse.

'Yes, Matt.'

'Then do it.' He scowled briefly at Kelly. 'So I guess you've seen something like this before?'

'Yes,' she replied, as they continued treating their patient.

'Breathing is becoming more rapid. Respiration distress evident. Intubate.' Kelly concentrated on her patient, although she registered Matt's body language. She knew he wasn't too happy with her taking over, but what was she supposed to do? She was doing what she thought was in the best interests of their patient. She couldn't help it if she had more A and E experience than him. After all, she'd been travelling the world for the past six years, working in different countries in a variety of situations. Matt, on the other hand, had done his training in Melbourne and had then returned to the rural subalpine village of Bright to join the family GP practice.

Once the patient had been intubated and the Haldol and Valium were working, Kelly was a lot happier with Mr Davidson's condition. His IV fluids had normalised his BP and the situation had turned from critical to stable.

'I'll organise his transfer to Wangaratta hospital.' Matt checked the ECG readings before ripping off his protective clothing and walking from the room.

Kelly grimaced with the way his back was ramrod straight again. Didn't the guy ever relax a little? Maybe during her six months here she could show Matthew Bentley that there was more to life than work, work, work. No. She wasn't here to flirt with her colleague. She was here to get away from the recent pressures that had swamped her life. If Matt wanted to work until he dropped, he could go right ahead. She, on the other hand, was determined to enjoy herself.

Kelly double-checked the patient's vital signs, glad to see Mr Davidson was now in a better condition. Hopefully, this little incident would convince him to give up the drugs completely, but she'd seen it before and, even after being revived from an overdose, many patients still continued to do hard drugs.

Kelly went into the little lunch-room, complete with kitchenette, only to find Matt sitting at the table, writing up the notes. Squaring her shoulders, she continued over to the urn and poured herself a cup of hot water. Dunking a teabag in it, she turned to face him, leaning against the bench.

'That went well,' she said, by way of opening up communication lines.

'Yes.' He continued to write.

'I gather he'll go by ambulance to Wangaratta?'

'Yes.'

'Interesting case, although I'm pretty sure he'll continue to do drugs.'

'Yes.'

'It irritates me when people don't learn from their mistakes. That guy is lucky to be alive, but do you think he'll see it that way?'

'Yes.'

Kelly frowned. Did Matt really think Mr Davidson would change? Or maybe Matt wasn't really listening to what she was saying. A twinkle of mischief light her eyes and she said in the same tone, 'So I guess we're having sex later tonight?'

'Yes—No!' His head jerked up and those dark blue eyes stared at her in disbelief. 'What?' He frowned, unsure he'd heard her correctly. Had she just suggested they have *sex*? His heartbeat increased at the thought and his gaze flicked briefly over her trim, taut and terrific body.

She looked even better out of the leathers, even though she was wearing baggy green cotton theatre scrubs.

She shifted from the bench, jiggling the teabag up and down in the cup as she slowly made her way towards him. He swallowed convulsively, unable to break his gaze. He felt his own blood pressure rise and clenched his jaw in an effort to control his body's unconscious reaction to her.

'You said yes.' Her voice was husky and he swallowed once more.

'I…er…I wasn't listening.'

'I know.' She put the cup on the table, then placed both hands palms down and leaned over, closing the distance between them.

'Kell—' He choked on her name before quickly clearing his throat. 'Kelly, you know you tricked me.'

'Oh, sure, but it was your subconscious answering the question. That means you're attracted to me.'

Matt stared into the emerald green depths of her eyes and

took a deep breath, that exotic spicy scent winding its way around him. He was a sucker for eyes. Gorgeous, green eyes. And hers were amazing. That, in itself, was a dangerous sign. Still, he decided to play along with her game, enjoying the momentary thrill. 'What if I am?'

'Then it's mutual.'

'It's crazy. We don't even know each other.'

'So? Haven't you ever done anything crazy in your life before?' Her tone was soft, seductive, and Matt responded to it. She could quite easily pick him up and push him over the edge—over the edge that had no reason or logic. And one thing he prided himself on was being logical.

'Reckless? Yes, but crazy?' He stood, edging closer—so close their breathing mingled. The tip of his nose brushed hers and if she puckered up her lips, they'd kiss. 'No.' He stayed there for a second longer, their gazes still melded together. She had eyes he could have drowned in and hair that he desperately wanted to plunge his fingers into. Her lips were practically begging him to kiss them but Matt drew on every last vestige of self-control and managed to pull away.

He collected his file and walked out of the room. Kelly slumped into a chair with relief. Wow! He was good. *Really* good. And sexy. *Really* sexy.

'You don't want this. You don't need this,' she said firmly to herself. 'You've been divorced for a whole six weeks and the last thing you need right now is to get involved with someone else.' Especially if that someone was her colleague for the next six months. He may be as delicious as a chocolate mud cake but eating a whole one could make a girl feel sick.

She rested her head on her hands, unable to forget that gleam of challenge she'd seen in his eyes. He'd admitted to being attracted to her and even though she wasn't interested in seriously dating someone, surely she could have a bit o fun loosening Matt up. The man seemed to be constantly frowning—well, when he looked at her anyway.

She would make him her 'project' while she was in town. After all, she had to focus on something to get her thought the next six months. Why not Matthew Bentley?

They had a steady tickle of patients arriving all night long, which surprised Kelly. As it was Saturday night, they'd even had the casualties from a bar-room brawl come in, two men requiring stitches in their hands.

A mother brought her child in, concerned because he wasn't breathing properly. Kelly watched as Matt took charge, speaking to the young boy of five with clear, calm authority. He seemed to know the child and the mother quite well, which wasn't surprising in a small country practice. For a brief moment a pang of envy engulfed her, but she brushed it away.

'You're very natural with children,' she remarked once the boy was settled, his breathing now under control.

'Thank you.' His tone was clipped, as though he wasn't interested in having a conversation with her. Kelly wasn't going to let that stop her as she followed him down the corridor to the nurses' desk. He sat in the chair and opened the case notes. Kelly leant against the edge of the desk and regarded him thoughtfully.

'Do you have any?'

He looked up at her, that frown fixed firmly in place. 'Any what?'

'Children.'

'No. I'm not married.'

'Since when do you have to be married to have children?'

Matt shook his head. 'Although many people don't find it necessary, I'm one of the old-fashioned types.'

Kelly nodded and smiled at him. 'So am I.'

'You are?' He was surprised and he wished she wouldn't

smile at him like that. It made it considerably harder for him to hold onto his resolve to keep her at arm's length.

'You seem surprised.'

'I just hadn't pegged you for that type.'

'Really? Then what type had you pegged me for?' She was very interested to hear his answer.

'The globe-trotting, no-strings-attached type of person.'

Kelly tilted her head to the side. 'You don't need to be single to trot the globe.'

It was then Matt recalled that she was recently divorced. 'True. Did you and your husband travel together?'

'Ex-husband. And, yes, we did. For five years. It's only been six weeks since we signed off on our divorce.' She shook her head, a curl coming loose from her bun. She tucked it behind her ear.

'No children?' he asked, mesmerised by the colour of her hair. It was so vibrant and deep. He watched as she looked down at her hands before shaking her head.

'No,' she said softly. 'No children.'

Matt was amazed at how vulnerable she appeared. Was this for real or was it an act? He opened his mouth to ask her another question but the phone rang and he quickly snatched up the receiver before it could wake any of their patients.

The buzzer for room three lit up and as the nurses who were on duty tonight were all busy, Kelly decided to go and see what one of the bar-room brawlers needed.

Several hours later, she changed into a pair of faded denim jeans, top and jumper before saying goodnight to the staff. Shrugging into her leather jacket, she held her helmet in one hand and jangled her keys with the other as she walked out into the cool, brisk July morning.

She saw Matt out the corner of her eye just as she was getting onto the bike. She scrambled off and rushed over to him. 'Hi. Long time, no see.'

He smiled politely and it made her more determined to get a genuine smile from him sooner rather than later.

'I was wondering if there was a good place you could recommend for breakfast. I thought there would be a few places open as a lot of the skiers will be eating up big before heading up the mountain.'

'There are.' His gaze roved over her briefly but remained expressionless. 'There's a bar and grill down the corner here…' He indicated down the street. 'Or the bakery is open but that's to the left and—'

'Why don't you join me?' Kelly asked. 'I'm hungry. You're, no doubt, hungry.' She shrugged. 'Let's do breakfast.' She felt him hesitate. 'Come on, Matt. It's not espionage, just breakfast, and if you come, I don't need to risk getting lost on my first morning here.'

He weighed up the pros and cons. If he went, he'd have to sit across the table from her, looking into her sexy eyes. The thought made him mildly uncomfortable, not because it was a bad prospect—quite the opposite. Then again, he could tell her more about the clinic and how things were run. It might be his one and only chance to set some ground rules, as well as suggesting she trade her motorbike in for a car during her stay.

'All right, then. Why don't we take my car?' He indicated the red four-wheel-drive he was standing next to. 'You can collect your bike on the way back.'

'Sounds good.' Kelly shoved the bike keys back into her pocket and waited impatiently for him to unlock the passenger door. 'This is going to be fun.'

'What were you and Dad thinking?' Matt asked his sister when he saw her on Monday afternoon. He'd spent most of Sunday catching up on sleep and hadn't been too impressed when visions of Kelly had invaded his dreams.

'About what?'

'About hiring Kelly O'Shea for this practice.'

'I don't see what the problem is, Matt. She's just what this practice needs. Even Dad agreed.'

'Kelly's been here less than seventy-two hours and already she'd upsetting the balance. Didn't you hear what she did to Mr Jorgensen's leg this morning?'

'No.'

'She treated his wound with honey! *Honey*!'

'So? Honey has been known to have healing properties. Besides, how do you know?'

'Because ever since she did, every patient who has been in here has been talking about it. I'm surprised your patients haven't mentioned it.'

Rhea shrugged. 'I'm interested to see if it works. Kelly has a lot of experience in different types of medicine so I guess we can expect the unexpected.'

'You can say that again,' Matt growled under his breath.

'I heard how she diagnosed that drug-addict patient in A and E on Saturday night. Sounded very impressive.'

'She was,' Matt acknowledged with a deep frown.

Rhea scrutinised her brother.

'What?' he asked, when he looked up and caught her staring.

'So you're a bit cautious of her because of her supposed unorthodox approach to medicine, is that it?'

Matt shrugged. 'There's something else but I can't put my finger on it.'

'I can.' Rhea smiled triumphantly. 'You're attracted to Kelly and *that's* what bothers you the most. Don't try and deny it, Matt,' she continued, and Matt leaned back in his chair, closing his eyes and massaging his temples. 'I know you like redheads.' Rhea paused and Matt looked at her again. 'Do you think she's like Jana or Louise? Only out for what she can get?'

'I don't know.' He shrugged, adding emphasis to his

words. 'We had breakfast yesterday morning after finishing at the hospital.'

'I know.'

'How do—? No, I don't think I want to know.'

'Small town, Matt. People gossip.'

'It was just breakfast but, see, this is what I mean. She's disturbing the status quo.'

'She's disturbing your routine, you mean. Matt, you're thirty-three and you're in such a rut.'

'I am not.' He stood up and turned his back on her, looking out the window. The sound of his sister's laughter drifted around the room.

'I don't blame you for being attracted to her. She's a very beautiful woman,' Rhea continued. 'Lovely red curls, bright blue eyes—'

'They're green,' he corrected automatically, turning around to face her.

'Gotcha!' Rhea clapped her hands in triumph.

Matt scowled at her. 'Got what?'

'You know her eye colour. So, anyway, what happened at breakfast?'

'I thought I'd tell her about the clinic, explain how things work. Maybe convince her to get rid of her motorbike.'

'And that didn't happen?'

'No.'

'Then what did?'

'We ate breakfast.' Matt scratched his head and Rhea laughed. 'She told me a bit about her travels and some of the interesting cases she'd seen. Then I found myself sharing some medical stories with her, and before I knew it, breakfast was over.'

'Matt, women don't need a reason to go out for breakfast—we simply love doing it.' She shrugged before crossing to his side. Placing her hand on his shoulder, she looked up at him. 'Promise me you won't tar Kelly with the same brush as Jana and Louise? She *is* different, Matt.'

'All I know is that dangerous, untouchable women and I don't mix.'

'So which category does Kelly fall into? Dangerous or untouchable?'

Matt looked tiredly at his sister. 'Let it go, Rhea. I've got patients to see. You've got patients to see.'

'Kelly's got patients to see,' Rhea continued. 'Yes, I know the drill.' She stretched.

'Good.' He was relieved she was going to let it drop.

'Although…'

Matt groaned and buried his head in his hands as his sister continued.

'I must say I *love* the way she dresses. Have you seen what she's wearing today?'

'Yes.' He wished he hadn't. If he'd thought the leathers had been provocative, they were nothing on the outfit she was wearing today. 'It's completely inappropriate for consulting.'

'What? It's neat, it's professional. Do you know who made that skirt she's wearing?'

'I don't care who made it, Rhea,' Matt blustered. 'It's inappropriate.'

'Why?' Rhea lifted her chin in challenge.

Matt clenched his jaw together. He wasn't going to tell his sister it was because it revealed far too much of her legs when she sat down or bent over. He'd almost hyperventilated at the sight.

The teasing light was back in Rhea's eyes. 'There's nothing wrong with *looking*, you know. She's single. You're single.'

'She's divorced,' he amended.

'That's right. That means she's single.'

'But her divorce was only signed a few weeks before she came here, or so she told me.'

'Discussing personal aspects of her life! Interesting. Very interesting.'

Matt groaned in frustration. The knock on his door was a welcome relief, but before he could reply, Kelly opened the door and breezed into the room, the black skirt in question swishing around her legs, the ruffled split up the front giving him teasing glimpses of her knees and inner thighs. Her siren-red shirt was unbuttoned just one too many, revealing the slightest bit of cleavage. Totally inappropriate for work, he fumed silently.

'Here are the case notes you wanted to look over, Matt.' She placed them on his desk before looking from him to Rhea and back again. She nodded slowly, 'Obviously I'm interrupting, and by the guilty looks on your faces, you were discussing me.'

A smile spread across her face and Matt felt his gut tightening in response. She was a very beautiful woman. It was a fact—pure and simple. He watched as her hand drifted down her side to where the edge of her shirt had come untucked. She used her thumb to push the fabric of her shirt beneath the black band, the action drawing attention to her slim waist as well as her breasts.

Matt swallowed convulsively, cross with himself for getting all hot under the collar only seconds after she'd entered the room. What on earth was wrong with him? He wasn't an adolescent! He should be able to control his hormones. But it seemed whenever Kelly was around, he was completely lost.

'Actually, we were,' Rhea admitted.

'Right. I'll leave you to it, then.' Kelly smiled as though she enjoyed being discussed then left the room, closing the door firmly behind her. And why *shouldn't* they discuss her? She was new here and they had every right to assess the

way she was fitting into their practice. It wasn't the first
time she'd been talked about and it wouldn't be the last.
'One of the perks,' she mumbled happily as she headed back
to her clinic room. After roaming the globe for the past five
years with her ex-husband, Freddy, both of them working
in six-monthly GP locum positions, Kelly was more than
used to being discussed.

Freddy! Boy, was she glad *that* part of her life was over.
Freddy had finally succumbed to the pressures from his family to join them in practice. Of course, a GP wasn't good
enough for *his* family, even with all the diplomas and extra
training they'd both done during their travels. No. Freddy's
parents had demanded he go back and study surgery.

His parents hadn't been pleased that Freddy had married
her, especially when after six years, Kelly had failed to produce an heir. As Freddy was their only son, they were re-
lying on him to carry on the family name. Little did it matter
that Freddy's sister had married a man they'd approved of
and had already produced three sons!

She honestly hoped he was happy. They were divorced
now and she had no regrets—well, except for one, but now
wasn't the time to dwell on it. She shrugged off her disbelief
at her own stupidity and sat down at her desk, flicking
through her next patient's notes before heading out to the
waiting room to call them through.

Her patient was a little boy of almost eighteen months,
who was holding onto his mother's hand as they walked
into the room. The mother sat him down beside her and
pulled out a toy car. He took it eagerly, rubbing his hands
over the toy, feeling the tactile sensations and spinning the
wheels.

Kelly smiled warmly at the mother. 'I'm Dr O'Shea. How
can I help you today, Lorraine?'

'It's Justin. He's still not sleeping well.'

Kelly glanced down at Justin's case notes before her and

scanned Matt's neat handwriting. Typical of him to write so clearly. He was such an intense man and a perfectionist, too. Illegibility would probably drive him crazy. She wondered how he would manage deciphering her appalling scrawl.

She reread the paragraph, annoyed that she was allowing her mind to wander while she was working. It appeared that little Justin wasn't having fun in the evenings, and by the look of his extremely tired mother, neither was she.

Kelly nodded. 'Why don't you tell me some more about it? How is he when he's sleeping? Is he fitful? Still and then all of a sudden writhing around in the bed? Or is he just waking up screaming for no reason?'

'He screams for no reason. It's getting to the stage where neither of us are sleeping and that's not good, Dr O'Shea.' Tears started to gather in Lorraine's eyes.

'What are his eating habits like?'

'He eats regularly—almost like clockwork—but there's not a lot of variety.'

'That's normal. Babies are born with four times the amount of tastebuds of adults so different tastes are really magnified with children. If what he's eating is healthy, then don't worry too much about variety. How is he socially? Do you go to a play group?'

'Yes. He seems fine with the other children but most of the time he just wants to be left alone. He likes playing with the toys and he's very clever at putting them into straight lines. He colour co-ordinates them, too, but on days like this, when he's overtired, he cries a lot and doesn't want to play with anyone.'

Kelly smiled. 'I doubt I'd want to play with anyone if I hadn't been getting enough sleep either.' She glanced down at the notes once more. 'I see that Dr Bentley prescribed some medicine to help Justin sleep through the night. How's that been going?'

Lorraine shook her head. 'I can't get it into him. He screams and gets himself so worked up that we both end up crying. It's just not working.'

'Have you tried putting the medicine into a drink before bedtime?'

'I can *do* that?'

'Sure. If that's the only way to get it into him, then give it a go, but that's only a short-term solution designed to let both you and Justin get some sleep. I take it there are just the two of you?' she asked softly, not wanting to tread on the other woman's toes.

'Yes. My boyfriend left me as soon as he knew I was pregnant. He wanted me to have an abortion but I couldn't. I just couldn't. I thought I could cope.' Tears started to stream down Lorraine's face. 'I thought I could…do…it.' She hiccuped.

Kelly came around her desk and reached for the box of tissues, offering one to Lorraine. She crouched down beside her. 'It's all right. You have a good cry. It can't be easy,' she soothed. 'And you're doing a great job. Justin isn't neglected nor unhappy, he's just not sleeping well. We're going to get to the bottom of this, I promise you.'

Lorraine continued to cry as Justin sat there, his legs stuck out in front of him, holding onto his toy. His eyes were focused straight ahead and his body was rocking slightly backwards and forwards. She wondered whether Matt was thinking about ordering other tests.

She needed to have a look at Justin's eyes but since both he and his mother were obviously exhausted, she decided to leave it for a few days. She'd discuss the situation with Matt before doing anything else.

'Listen, try putting that medicine into his drink tonight and call me tomorrow to let me know how it went. If it works well, do the same tomorrow night and then come and see me the next day when you're both refreshed. How's that sound?'

'What if I can't get him to drink it?'

'Let me know either way. If that doesn't work, we'll try something else. We'll figure this out, Lorraine, but first we need both of you to get a good night's sleep. That's our first priority.' Kelly rubbed her hand soothingly along Lorraine's back before standing up.

'Come on, Justin,' Lorraine said, after she'd blown her nose and wiped her tears. 'Home time.' She put the bag on her shoulder before picking up her son.

Kelly watched the little boy closely, noting he didn't look at either herself or his mother, his fingers rubbing furiously on the toy he was holding. When they'd gone, she sat down and wrote up her notes. 'Interesting. Very interesting.'

Kelly started to feel rotten as the afternoon wore on. Her feet ached, her head ached and her stomach felt as though she'd been on hundreds of dizzy rides. She must be coming down with something as she'd felt this way two days ago.

Then again, she had seen a lot of people suffering from flu. Perhaps it was her turn. Still, it wasn't a good way to start a new job. She took some paracetamol, which eased her headache slightly, but the cup of tea she'd had an hour ago wasn't sitting too well. Maybe the milk had been off. That was probably it.

Once the clinic was finished, she wrote up her notes and said goodbye to Bianca, the receptionist, before walking across the road to the middle house.

She dumped her bag at the door and continued to the bathroom, shedding her clothes as she went, eager to stand beneath the hot, soothing spray of the shower. She'd only been in the shower for a few minutes when a wave of nausea overwhelmed her and she sank to the bottom of the stall, her legs unable to support her any longer.

Kelly waited until it passed, glad that she hadn't been

physically ill, and finally crawled her way back up the wall.
'So much for relaxing,' she muttered, as she turned the taps
off and started to towel herself dry. When she was dressed
in boxer shorts and top, she headed straight for bed. There,
she wearily combed her tight curls, which framed her face
and shoulders, using up all her energy drying them as best
she could.

With them still slightly damp, she tied her hair up on the
top of her head so it wouldn't get in the way and snuggled
into the pillow, sleep claiming her instantly.

The buzzing of the doorbell woke her. She lay in bed for
a few seconds, eyes open as she tried to get her bearings.
That's right, she was in Bright. As the doorbell buzzed
again, she groaned, her headache returning.

'Kelly? Kelly?'

It was Matt.

Dragging herself out of bed on legs that felt like lead, she
stumbled over the clothing she'd dropped earlier and finally
opened the door. 'What?'

'Kelly? What's wrong?' Matt was instantly inside and
shutting the door behind him, blocking out the cool night
air. 'Your face is pale and your eyes are like slits.' The rest
of her, however, looked irresistibly sexy and he couldn't
help the burst of desire that flooded through him.

Most of her hair was tied up in an unruly mass on top of
her head while little wisps and tendrils that had escaped
bounced around her shoulders. The boxer shorts, which revealed most of her gorgeous legs, and the loose-fitting top
only fuelled the spark of desire even more.

'Really? Usually they're closed when I sleep.'

'You were asleep?'

'Sure. I do it every night—well, most of the time. When
I'm not on call. You know the drill.' She was so fatigued
she felt punch drunk.

'Have you taken something? A sleeping tablet or something?' He placed his hands on either side of her face and tilted her head back so he could look into her eyes.

'No.' She shook herself free from his touch. Even in this drowsy state she registered the warmth of his skin against hers and how wonderful it felt. 'Did you want something?' she asked as she headed back towards her bedroom.

He followed her, picking up her clothes as he went. Matt watched as Kelly climbed back into bed and rested her head thankfully against the pillow. Something wasn't right. He dropped the clothes into the laundry basket before washing his hands. He picked up the towels she'd used off the floor as well. Was she always this messy?

He returned to find her breathing deeply in and out. She'd gone back to sleep! He frowned and placed his hand on her forehead. She didn't appear to have a temperature. Perhaps the last few days were catching up with her. It couldn't be easy, changing jobs every six months. He knew he could never do it. Yet that was the way Kelly chose to live her life, even if he didn't understand it.

It was only half past eight and he wondered whether she'd had anything to eat. He headed into the kitchen but found it empty except for the breakfast dishes, which had been left in the sink. She hadn't even bothered to rinse them and now the cereal she'd eaten about fourteen hours earlier had set rock hard around the edge of the bowl.

Matt turned on the tap and quickly washed the dishes. Next he made a sandwich, wrapped it up and put it in the fridge. He filled the kettle and put a teabag in a cup, ready for her next cuppa. He checked the heating thermostat as well as ensuring the doors and windows were locked.

He'd come over to apologise for the way he and his sister had been talking about her, although from the way she'd laughed off the matter, she obviously hadn't minded. Still, *he* felt bad about it and that had been enough motivation for him to apologise.

Matt walked back to her room and watched her sleep. She looked small beneath the thick, winter covers, her red curls vibrant against the whiteness of the pillow-slip.

The crack she'd made the other day about them having sex had produced vivid images in his mind which had stayed there ever since. He knew she'd only been joking but… He raked a hand through his hair in frustration. Even the mere mention of it had been enough to disturb his sleep last night.

Why had she even put the suggestion into his mind in the first place? It was then he acknowledged that she hadn't. Ever since he'd first laid eyes on her, he'd felt a tightening in his gut and his hormones stir. She was extremely attractive and, as Rhea had pointed out that afternoon, there was no harm in looking. And looking was all he intended to do.

He'd learnt his lesson about untouchable women. They weren't for him. He needed someone who would live the quiet life with him here in Bright, and be happy to help him raise a family. Kelly wasn't that person, he was sure of it. There could never be anything more than a working relationship between them and he was determined to make sure of it—even though he'd be fighting himself every step of the way.

CHAPTER TWO

KELLY woke some time around two a.m. and, after slipping her feet into her warm, sheepskin-lined slippers, shuffled to the kitchen. It was nice and warm but right now she was starving. She switched the kettle on, surprised to find a cup ready for her to use.

She glanced around the kitchen. The dishes were done. Walking to the fridge to get the milk, she was surprised to find a sandwich sitting there, just begging her to eat it. What had happened? Had the fairies come? They hadn't visited her since her last tooth had fallen out. Why now? She ran her tongue over her teeth, just to double-check.

'Oh, well. Whoever did all this—thank you.'

She took the sandwich and her cup of tea back to bed and climbed beneath the warm covers. Flicking on the television she'd carried in from one of the other rooms, she sat up in bed, munching and drinking, quite satisfied with how she was feeling. Obviously she'd just needed a bit of sleep. Half an hour later she was tired again and, after brushing her teeth, she headed back to bed.

When Kelly woke in the morning, she felt worse than before. She sat up slowly and swung her legs over the side of the bed. When the world had stopped revolving, she tried standing, only to find her legs had turned to jelly. Leaning against the wall for support, she felt a churning in her stomach and decided she'd better pick the pace up a little or she wouldn't make it to the bathroom in time.

Thankfully she did, but as she rinsed her mouth out and brushed her teeth, Kelly looked at her reflection with concern. Something was wrong and it was only getting worse.

Her face was deathly pale, her eyes looked sunken and exhausted, yet she'd just woken from quite a good sleep.

Had there been something wrong with the sandwich the fairies had left? Or perhaps it was something completely different from food poisoning or the flu. On shaky legs, she made it to the front door where she'd left her bag the night before. Carrying it through to the lounge room, she sat down and opened it up, taking out her personal diary.

She flicked back through the pages, looking for the day her last cycle had begun.

Eight weeks ago! The book started to tremble in her hands as she turned over a few more pages to the day before her divorce—right in the middle of her cycle. She'd spent that night with Freddy, believing him when he'd said he'd wanted to try and see if the magic was still there. The next morning, they'd signed the divorce papers with no one knowing about the events of the previous evening.

Kelly had just wanted the divorce over and done with, especially after the way Freddy had admitted he'd wanted one last fling with her. How could she have been so stupid as to believe him? She couldn't be pregnant. It was impossible, or at least that's what the gynaecologist had told her when she'd been diagnosed with endometriosis at seventeen. It had taken her years to come to terms with the fact that she was barren and after five years of marriage to Freddy, who'd had a low sperm count, not one single pregnancy had resulted. So it was impossible that this last fling would have left a lasting impression.

Her cycle had more than likely been thrown out because of the divorce and the change in job. Kelly clung to that as she showered and dressed for work. If it wasn't pregnancy, then maybe she should see a specialist and get herself checked out again, but it had only been three months since she'd had the last lot of adhesions removed from her ovaries.

Then again, it couldn't hurt to do a pregnancy test. At least then she could definitely cross it off the list. She decided to get across to the clinic early to do the test before any of her patients arrived, but another bout of nausea made her late.

She saw three patients, finding it more difficult than usual to push her personal thoughts aside. She almost kissed Bianca when she announced one of Kelly's patients had cancelled. Closing her consulting-room door, she took out the test with mixed feelings of excitement and trepidation. Her hands were shaking as she slipped on a pair of gloves and pulled out the urine specimen she'd done earlier that morning.

After performing the test, she checked the clock. A few minutes. All she had to do was to wait a few minutes and then she would know. She packed everything away, glancing at the test every few seconds to see if there was a result.

Never in her life had time stood as still as it was doing now. Impatience got the better of her and she paced around the room in an effort to control it. 'Hurry up, hurry up,' she repeated but when the time was up, she found it difficult to look. Finally, she opened her eyes and stared down at the test.

'Positive!' Kelly slumped down into her chair in shock. She was pregnant!

Matt knocked briefly on Kelly's consulting-room door before entering. He already knew she didn't have a patient with her as he'd checked with Bianca. He closed the door behind him, noticing she hadn't moved.

As soon as he started walking towards her, she jerked her head up and stared at him. Her face was pale and the green eyes that were usually full of life were now glassy as she stared almost unseeingly at him.

'Kelly?' He crossed to her side. 'Are you all right?'

She took a deep breath before meeting his gaze. 'I'm fine. Just a bit tired.' She forced a smile.

'Are you sure? You didn't look too good when I called around last night.'

She frowned at him. 'Last night?'

'Don't you remember?'

'No. Sorry. Was it you who did my dishes and made that sandwich?'

'Yes.'

'Thank you.'

'You were sleeping pretty soundly.' Matt watched her as she shuffled bits of paper around her desk and then he noted the pregnancy test. 'Who's pregnant?' he asked.

'What?'

'The pregnancy test.' He gestured to it. 'Who's pregnant?'

'Oh—just a tourist. Someone passing through.'

'Ah.' He nodded. 'First-time mum-to-be?'

'Yes, as a matter of fact.'

'Single or married?'

'What does it matter?' Kelly rounded on him with such force that he took a step back. 'Sorry.' She sighed and massaged her temples with her fingertips. 'I'm sorry, Matt. I've just been a little…off colour lately.'

'You should have said something.'

She heard the instant concern in his tone and felt even worse.

'I'll change the on-call roster until you're feeling better.'

'No, it's all right. I—'

'Rhea and I can handle things for a while until you're better,' he continued when she tried to protest. 'It's been done before. Doctors aren't immune to being sick, you know.' He smiled at her—a real smile—and it was her undoing. He was being so nice and kind. Tears filled her eyes and she nodded.

'Thanks,' she whispered.

'Hey.' He reached for a tissue but instead of holding it out to her, as she'd expected, he came close and dabbed gently at her eyes. 'You should have said something sooner. You may have just started working here but we do understand that you hadn't planned to get sick.'

'No,' she said glumly, as the tears began to fall. 'Thank you for being so nice.' Her hormones were in such a state that she couldn't stop herself from crying.

'Kelly.' He pulled her into his arms, stroking her curls. In that instant, he admitted to himself that this was something he'd wanted to do ever since she'd pulled up on that ridiculous motorbike.

Kelly took a deep breath, the scent of his aftershave filling her senses. The warmth of his body pressed against hers was all she'd imagined and more. Since she'd arrived, she'd teased him, admired him and bossed him around, yet here he was, offering compassion, holding her close to him as though she was someone to be cherished.

Never had Kelly felt so…so…content in her life. With Matt's arms around her, she felt as though everything just *had* to turn out right—but nothing would turn out right, especially if she was pregnant.

She needed further confirmation. The test she'd done could have shown a false positive. She'd do a blood test and send it off for confirmation. That was the only way to go.

With this thought, her tears started to subside. The mind was a powerful thing and although she'd had other symptoms of pregnancy, she'd known of cases where the mind constantly played tricks on the body, making it think it was pregnant. Perhaps that was what was happening to her!

She hiccuped and reluctantly pulled back. To her delight, Matt didn't drop his arms completely but brought his hands up to rest on her shoulders as he looked down at her.

'Feeling better?'

'Yes. Thank you.' She sniffed and gave him a watery smile.

Matt brushed a stray tear from her cheek with the back of his knuckles, his hand then resting against her cheek, cupping her face. Tenderly, his thumb brushed over her lips and she gasped at the intimate contact.

His gaze flicked momentarily down to her mouth before meeting her gaze once more. Kelly couldn't believe the desire she read in his eyes. Butterflies churned in her stomach, a more welcome sensation than the nausea which had been plaguing her.

Her tongue darted out to wet her lips just as his thumb brushed over them again. The two connected and when Matt groaned with pleasure it was Kelly's undoing. Even though she'd told herself she wasn't looking for another relationship, she couldn't resist opening her mouth wider and kissing his thumb.

Slowly she nibbled, drawing it further into her mouth, and Matt thought he might pass out from the surge of ecstasy that passed through him. When she sucked sweetly, he moaned again and closed his eyes. He couldn't believe the way this woman was making him feel, but one thing he knew for sure—he didn't want her to stop.

Kelly wasn't sure what excited her more—the feel of Matt's thumb inside her mouth or that he was standing before her, his eyes closed, loving every second of what she was doing to him.

He slowly pulled his thumb back, caressing it over her parted lips before his eyes opened and he gazed down at her. Both of them were breathing hard and fast, only wanting fulfillment of what they'd inadvertently started.

'Kelly.' His deep voice washed over her and she sighed as his other hand edged its way up her neck so her face was cradled in both his hands. With agonising slowness, he started to lower his head. Her heart was pounding so furiously against her ribs, she was positive he could hear it.

Bzzzz. 'Your next patient has arrived, Kelly.' Bianca's voice came over the intercom and it was enough to break the intimate little bubble which had captured them both. Bianca was waiting for an answer. All Kelly knew was that she wanted the world to stop revolving while she and Matt finished what they'd started, but one look into those hypnotic blue eyes of his revealed he'd already withdrawn.

Matt's hands dropped back to his sides and he took two huge steps back. He pointed to her intercom. 'I'll let you get back to work.' He pivoted on his heel, opened the door and walked out, directly into his own consulting room. He shut the door, leaning against it for a moment, trying to desperately come to grips with what had just happened.

Somehow, Kelly O'Shea had managed to get under his skin like an…an annoying splinter, one that was going to be hard and, no doubt, painful to remove. How could he have lost control like that? She was a wanderer—a person who liked change, who travelled and moved around. He was the opposite. Travelling on holiday was fine, but he didn't like change—especially when it involved him losing sight of his resolution, and that was exactly what had just happened between himself and Kelly.

It disturbed him—*she* disturbed him—far too much. Knowing she could make him forget. Knowing she had that sort of hold over him. He didn't like it. He'd only been offering her a bit of compassion. How had things escalated so far and so fast?

He shook his head as he stormed over to his desk and yanked his medical bag onto the table. He went through the routine check to make sure he had everything he needed for the house calls he was about to make and was glad that work still seemed to be able to help him focus more clearly.

*   *   *

Kelly couldn't believe how exhausted she was by the end of the day. It was worse than yesterday when she dragged herself into the sanctuary of her bedroom, collapsing on the bed with relief. She'd managed to take a blood sample from her arm that afternoon and now all she had to do was wait.

As she curled up in bed, she rested a hand on her flat stomach, wondering if indeed there really was a baby inside. A feeling of amazement washed over her and she gently moved her hand in small circles. 'Are you in there?' she whispered.

She might be pregnant! She might be about to have a baby! It was…a miracle.

The magnitude of the situation hit her with full force and tears of wonderment filled her eyes. It was something she'd only ever dreamed about, knowing it could never be a reality. So what had happened? How had she conceived? Between herself and Freddy, they'd had enough problems for them never to conceive. How had this happened?

'Freddy!' she gasped, and opened her eyes, her previous tranquillity shattered. If she really was pregnant then she'd need to tell Freddy. She knew exactly how he'd react. He'd want to remarry and want her to move to Melbourne to live with him, comforted in the bosom of his family. His parents, however, would probably just want her to hand over the child, especially if it was a boy, so *they* could raise him.

'No way.' Kelly shook her head emphatically and closed her eyes again. She stroked her stomach reassuringly. 'I would never let you be raised by those hypocritical snobs.' The possessive maternal instinct struck her with force. It was something she'd never thought she'd feel and now she had, she realised she desperately wanted this baby. It was too precious for her to let go of and she would fight for this child with everything she had.

'*If* you're pregnant,' she said firmly. Knowing she was getting ahead of herself, Kelly focused on relaxing. She reflected on her day, pleased that Lorraine had called through with the news that little Justin had drunk the medicine and they'd both had a good night's sleep. She still needed to discuss Justin with Matt as she wanted to order some extra tests. There were a few possibilities regarding Justin's condition but she wanted Matt's opinion before she went any further.

Matt. Gorgeous Matt, who'd shown her such compassion this morning. Kelly had no idea how things had become so out of control and was sure Matt was probably beating himself up for it. She liked the way he was all noble and gentlemanly. 'Chivalry,' she murmured sleepily and sighed, visions of Matt holding her firmly in his arms accompanying her as she drifted off to sleep.

She woke late the next morning and as she scrambled out of bed, Kelly felt herself swoon again. She stumbled into the wall, reminding herself that she had to get up more slowly in future. It must be a sign. She just had to be pregnant. All pregnant women swooned and fainted—well, at least they did in the movies.

She grinned to herself as she walked into the kitchen and opened the fridge, but the instant she saw food, her stomach churned in disgust. Clamping a hand over her mouth, she raced for the bathroom and emerged a few minutes later, feeling a bit better.

'Definitely pregnant,' she murmured as she sagged back onto her bed. Every muscle in her body ached. She pulled the covers up to her chin and lay there, trying to decide what to do next. If she *wasn't* pregnant, she should call in sick, otherwise she would risk passing her germs onto her patients and they weren't coming to the doctor's to *get* sick!

The blood test wouldn't be back in until later that afternoon…but she could always phone through to the lab later that morning and get the results.

'Yes.' The thought made her feel better and she tossed

the covers aside. She moved slowly, swinging her legs over before sitting up. She waited for her head to stop spinning before she stood. The sooner she had the results of that blood test, the sooner she'd know what course of action to take. In the meantime, she was sure she'd feel much better after a shower. They were expecting her and, apart from the nausea and muscle aches, she wasn't feeling too bad.

She headed for the phone and contacted the clinic. 'Sorry, Bianca,' Kelly said when the receptionist answered. 'I'm running late. I'll be there in ten minutes—less, hopefully.' Thank goodness work was only across the street.

She rang off and leaned her hand against the wall for support as she headed for the bathroom. The shower was nice and hot and she realised after a few minutes that her aches dulled slightly beneath the spray. 'Definitely pregnant,' she told herself again.

By the time she arrived at the clinic she was exhausted and slumped down into her consulting chair with relief.

As the morning progressed, Kelly discovered another problem. Her bladder seemed to have developed a mind of its own and although she felt slightly dehydrated and was drinking more water than usual, surely it wouldn't cause her to go to the toilet in between *every* patient she saw!

She was never more grateful when she said goodbye to her last patient for the morning and finally relaxed into her comfy chair. She leaned her head back and closed her eyes, glad of the momentary peace and quiet.

She should take this opportunity to call the lab before anyone else walked through her door. She sat forward and reached for the phone, hesitating. She'd been waiting for this moment all morning, but now it had arrived her emotions were mixed. What if she wasn't pregnant? What if it was just a figment of her imagination?

'Stop second guessing and find out,' she told herself briskly. Locating the number for the lab, she placed the call.

She had to wait six rings for someone to pick it up, and each ring had seemed to drag on for ever. She told them who she was and what she was looking for.

'Let me see,' the man on the other end of the phone said, his mouth obviously full of food. 'Dr Kelly O'Shea…' She could hear him riffling through pieces of paper. 'OK. Result is positive. Congratulations, you're pregnant.' His tone was uninterested and droll. 'Was there anything else?'

'Ah…no,' Kelly managed to croak, her eyes instantly filling with tears of joy at the news. She cleared her throat. 'That's it. Thank you.'

Kelly tenderly replaced the receiver and reached for a tissue. She sniffled with delight and blew her nose. She was pregnant. She was pregnant! By some miracle, she, Kelly O'Shea, was pregnant. She cried—tears of utter joy. There was a baby growing inside her. Something she'd thought would never, ever happen.

She placed her hands against her flat abdomen and smiled. 'Hello,' she whispered. 'It's your mummy here.' The words brought on a fresh bout of tears and she laughed as she wiped them away.

At the brisk knock at her door, Kelly sniffed and reached for another tissue, blowing her nose as the door was opened. Please, don't let it be Matt, she silently prayed, and sighed with relief when Rhea walked in.

'Kelly, I was wondering if you—' Rhea stopped and looked at her. 'What's wrong?'

'Nothing. Nothing. I'm fine.'

'Are you sure?' Rhea placed her hand on Kelly's forehead. 'You don't feel warm. Stick out your tongue.'

'I'm fine,' Kelly reiterated on a laugh.

'Stick out your tongue,' Rhea demanded, and Kelly obliged. 'That looks fine, too. So why is your make-up smudged and your nose glowing like Rudolf's?'

'Just some news I've received—*good* news,' she added.

'Are you sure? Matt said you weren't feeling too well yesterday.' Rhea settled into a chair.

'I'm fine.' Kelly shifted in her chair, the action sending ripples down to her bladder. 'Excuse me.' She slowly stood. 'I need to visit the little girls' room.'

'Again?'

'You're keeping score?' Kelly asked, noticing the way Rhea was watching her but nevertheless heading for the toilets. When she returned to her consulting room, Rhea was sitting in the same spot, patiently waiting her return. Kelly closed her door, realising Rhea was the type of person who didn't let go once they got their teeth into something.

'Let's review the facts,' Rhea said, her fingers steepled together, a look of determination on her face. 'You told Matt you weren't feeling well, you slept in this morning and have been constantly visiting the bathroom. You've been teary but in a happy way, and you've just received some good news. You have a jug of water and dry crackers on your desk which you've obviously been nibbling at all morning due to the fact that you're probably nauseated.'

Kelly nodded and waited.

'All of these point to morning sickness, which means you're pregnant.'

'Very impressive, Rhea. I can see why you make such a wonderful doctor and I don't see why I should look any further than you for my prenatal care.'

'Thank you, I'd be delighted. But the question remains…who's the father?'

'Freddy. My ex-husband. Look.' She waved away any thought of Freddy. 'I don't want to discuss this now. I've only just had confirmation that I am indeed pregnant and I need time to get used to it, as well as finding a way to get up in the mornings,' she grumbled as she took another sip of her water.

'Peppermint tea worked well for me,' Rhea said. 'I'll bring some over tonight.'

'Thanks. I'd appreciate that.'

There was another knock on her door and Matt walked in. 'Here you two are. Rhea, I've just added another patient to your afternoon house call list.'

'Gee, thanks.' Rhea stood and looked at Kelly. 'I'll see you later and we'll talk more.'

Kelly didn't miss the point Rhea was trying to make— that being, she wanted to know *everything*. She nodded. 'I look forward to it.' Rhea left and she half expected Matt to leave, too, but he didn't.

'Feeling better today?'

'Yes, thanks.'

'Good.' He stayed where he was by the door as though he didn't trust himself—or her. Their gazes held for a few seconds and the atmosphere in the room thickened dramatically. It was there, between them. The awareness, the attraction…and another man's baby.

It was enough to help her look away. She studied her desk and heard him move. He was leaving. Kelly searched for something to say and finally remembered about young Justin. 'Uh, Matt, have you got a minute?' she asked.

'Sure.'

'It's about young Justin. You saw him last week.'

He nodded. Feeling more comfortable that she wanted to talk about a patient, Matt closed the door and sat down in the seat his sister had just vacated. 'What's been happening?'

'Well, when Lorraine came in the other day, she said she couldn't get Justin to take the medicine you'd prescribed.'

'Phenergan.'

'Yes. I suggested she put it in his drink. She did and it worked.'

'Great.'

'Matt, I think there may be more going on with Justin than just a bad sleeping pattern.'

'Go on.'

'When he's been to see you in the past, how has he reacted?'

'Like any other normal toddler. He sits down and plays with the toys while I talk to Lorraine and then I examine him. Why?'

'How does he play with the toys?'

Matt frowned. 'I haven't really noticed.'

'He's coming to see me this afternoon. I'd like you to do the consult with me, if you don't mind.'

'No but can you give me a clue as to what you're looking for?'

'Epilepsy? Hearing problems? I noticed when he was here the other day that he didn't make eye contact with me, but as they were both so tired, I thought it best to deal with the sleep problem first before doing anything else.'

'Hmm.' He nodded again. 'What time is he due?'

Kelly consulted her schedule. 'Half past three.'

'I'll get Bianca to buzz me when he's in with you and come in as soon as I can.'

'Thanks.'

Matt stood and walked over to the door. He stopped and turned to face her. 'You sure you're feeling OK?'

Kelly smiled. 'I'm fine.'

'You still look pale.'

'It's winter. Everyone looks pale in winter,' she jested, hoping to get him off the track. There was no way she was going to tell him she was pregnant—not right this second at any rate. She would do it later, of course, but she needed more time to adjust to this big development in her life.

He nodded before closing her door behind him. Matt didn't believe her for one instant and it grated him for a number of reasons. The first one was that her reaction was similar to his own whenever he was sick. He denied it, he said he was all right and he soldiered on. He admired her for that, and at the moment he was trying to avoid having positive feelings towards Kelly O'Shea.

The other reason was that she might be passing her germs onto the patients and that wasn't good. It was usually the only way his mother had been able to override his own stubbornness when he'd been sick. 'You'll only make the patients worse if you go to work coughing and sneezing like that all day long,' she would say in her no-nonsense motherly tone.

Matt headed into his own consulting room and sat down. Come to think of it, he *hadn't* seen Kelly coughing or sneezing. Sure she was tired and exhausted, but not flu-type sick. Perhaps it was something else? Perhaps she was having her period. That had to be it. That was why she was probably playing things down. Women often did that.

He took a deep breath, glad he'd figured out a logical reason for her erratic behaviour. She was soldiering on because that's what women did, *and* she wasn't contagious. He had no need to feel concerned about her and could therefore put yesterday's episode down to her being hormonal.

'Logic.' He nodded. There was a logical reason for everything—except his unexpected attraction to Kelly.

CHAPTER THREE

KELLY had just welcomed Lorraine and Justin into her consulting room when Matt knocked and walked in.

'Hi, Lorraine.' He smiled. 'Kelly's asked me to stop by and say hello.' He crouched down to where Justin was standing next to his mother, his attention focused on his favourite toy car. 'Hello, Justin. Feeling better today?'

Justin didn't respond at all, refusing to divert his attention. It wasn't anything out of the ordinary. Eighteen-month-old toddlers often didn't respond to adults because they were shy or tired or just couldn't be bothered. Still, Kelly had a feeling it wasn't any of those things.

'Justin, honey.' Lorraine tapped him on the shoulder. 'Say hello to Doctor Matt.'

Justin glanced up at his mother and then at Matt before returning his attention to his car.

'I'm sorry,' Lorraine apologised. 'I'm trying to concentrate on his manners and it gets rather frustrating at times.'

'You'll get there,' Kelly encouraged. 'Have a seat.' Matt sat next to Lorraine with Justin dropping to the floor and spinning the wheels of his car. She knew Matt would be taking in every move the boy made and analysing it. Kelly brought her chair out from behind her desk so they were all sitting in a funny-shaped circle with Justin on the floor in the middle. 'How are things going, Lorraine? Sleeping better?'

The young mother nodded emphatically. 'The last two nights have been heaven. Justin's still been sleeping in my bed but at least we've both slept.'

'Good. It's fine to use the Phenergan once in a while but

not all the time. The most I'd recommend using it would be two nights straight, which is what you've done.'

'None tonight?' she asked.

'None tonight,' Kelly confirmed.

'All right. So what's next?'

'Well, I have a few theories as to why Justin might be having trouble sleeping, and I'd like to organise some tests for him.'

'What kind of tests?' There was a wary note in Lorraine's voice and her eyes were wide with concern.

'First of all, I'd like Justin to have an EEG. That's an electroencephalogram to test for epilepsy.'

'Epilepsy? But why? There's no history of epilepsy in my family and Justin has never had one of those convulsive fits or whatever they're called.'

'What about his father? Is there a history of epilepsy in his family?'

Lorraine bit her lip and shook her head as Kelly's words sank in. 'I don't know. He…he never said but…well…' She sighed. 'I don't know,' she repeated, a hint of helplessness in her tone.

'Epilepsy is a physical indication of an abnormal electrical discharge in the brain. Now, although this sounds scary, it's also, for the most part, a very controllable condition.'

'You mean drugs?'

'Medications nowadays are very good for controlling it, yes.'

'I don't want Justin to be on medication for the rest of his life.'

'I understand and perhaps we're jumping the gun a little. The EEG is just one test I'd like to do. I'd also like Justin to have a hearing test.'

'Hearing? His hearing is good.'

Kelly watched as Lorraine looked down at her son. He was still holding his car, spinning the wheels and feeling its surface. It wasn't normal. Most little boys, even before the age of eighteen months, would be pushing the car along the ground, making brm-brm noises.

'Lorraine,' Matt said gently, 'these are only general tests. We need to find out if there's something wrong with Justin and why he's not sleeping properly.'

'But I thought it was because he was in a bad routine. The other mothers at play group have done controlled crying with their children and been successful, but it doesn't seem to work with Justin. I know they think I'm a bad mother and as most of them are married…it just makes it that much worse to bear that I'm a single mother.' Tears had gathered in Lorraine's eyes while she'd been speaking and Matt quickly reached over and grabbed the box of tissues from Kelly's desk, offering one to her.

'You're not a bad mother,' he said firmly. 'You're here, asking for help, and we're going to give it to you. The tests Kelly's suggesting are routine for children with sleep problems. Something is wrong with Justin, we just don't know what. But we're absolutely determined to find out. Aren't we, Kelly?'

'Definitely.'

'So you're not sure what's wrong?'

'No, but by doing these tests, we can start crossing things off the list. Once we know what we're dealing with, we can move forward with a treatment plan. Now, I can't say what that treatment plan will be until we have a diagnosis. Our first step was to get you both some sleep so you could function and think more clearly. Now that that's done, I'd like to get the EEG done as soon as possible before you start having more bad nights.'

Lorraine was silent for a moment before nodding. 'What is an EEG again?'

'An electroencephalogram. What we'll be doing is placing pairs of electrodes in contact with Justin's scalp and it shows us what type of electrical activity is occurring in the brain. You might have seen it on some of the television medical shows where the reading comes out on a thin piece of paper and it looks as though someone's drawn a big scribble right down the middle.'

Lorraine nodded. 'Yeah. Yeah, I've seen that.'

'That's the readout from the EEG. That's the information we need. The test is very sensitive and will give us an accurate reading of what's happening to Justin's brain activity.'

Lorraine's bottom lip quivered. 'OK.' She turned to look at Matt. 'If you both think this is the best way to go, sure, I'll do it. I love my son.' Tears started to fall again. 'I just want him to be normal.'

Kelly bit her tongue. She wasn't sure Lorraine's wish would come true. Then again, people had different definitions of the word 'normal.' She just hoped Lorraine's perceptions would change if necessary.

'I'll organise the test for tomorrow morning. Is that all right with you, Matt?'

'I'll be there,' he confirmed.

'We'll do it at Bright hospital and I'll get Bianca to ring through the time to you.'

'What about the hearing test?'

'I can organise that,' Matt answered. 'I have a friend at Wangaratta hospital who can help us out.'

'Wangaratta? I have to take Justin into Wangaratta? That's a forty-five-minute drive from here. You can't do the test in the clinic?'

'We do have a hearing test here but, given Justin's age, I doubt we'd keep the headphones on him long enough to get an accurate reading. So, unfortunately, it's either Wangaratta hospital or Melbourne, which is almost four hours from here.'

'Justin just doesn't like different places,' Lorraine advised, bending down to pick her son up off the floor. She cradled him possessively and kissed the top of his head. Justin didn't seem to mind the action but squirmed a little into a better position. Lorraine held him tight, which he seemed to also like.

'I know this is all a lot for you to take in, Lorraine, and if you've got questions, which I'm sure you will once the information's had time to filter through, give either Matt or myself a call,' Kelly encouraged.

'That's right. We're here to help both you and Justin get through this.'

'What about tonight? You said no medicine. What should I do if he has another screaming fit?' As her own words penetrated, Lorraine's mouth hung open. 'He *has* had fits but just not in the way I thought.' Fresh tears welled and she held him tighter. 'Oh, no. Oh, no. What am I going to do?'

'Hey,' Kelly soothed as she crossed to the woman's side and placed her arm around her shoulders. 'You'll be fine. You're strong. You're a survivor or you wouldn't have made it this far on your own.'

'But what about Justin? He's not normal, is he? He's not normal and he never will be.'

'Don't compare apples and oranges. Justin is normal for Justin,' Matt said softly. 'That's what you've got to accept, and it isn't going to be easy.'

'For tonight, try doing what you've done the last two nights. Give him a drink as though there were medicine in it, let him sleep in your bed if that's what he's been doing.'

'I know he shouldn't but it's just easier.'

'That's fine. We can cross the bridge of getting him back into his own bed later. What's important now is for both of you to get a good night's sleep, without the help of medication.'

After blowing her nose one last time, Lorraine nodded

resolutely. Justin climbed off her knee, still concentrating on the wheels of his car.

'We'll figure it out.' Kelly stood and helped Lorraine up. 'I'll organise that appointment for tomorrow and get Bianca to phone the details through to you.'

'All right. Thank you.' Lorraine smiled a watery smile at them both. 'For everything. Come on Justin. Home time.'

'That's what we're here for,' Matt replied as he walked over to the door and held it open for her. When they were gone, he shut it again and turned to face Kelly.

'You're right. I was watching him carefully the whole time and there's definitely something wrong. I think it might be his hearing.'

'Because he didn't respond when you said hello?' Kelly manoeuvred her chair back behind her desk.

'Well that and the loud car that roared passed the surgery. I also dropped my pen to the floor while you and Lorraine were talking, and Justin didn't shift his focus from spinning those wheels.'

'Really? I don't remember you dropping your pen and on these wooden floor boards it would make a bit of noise. Perhaps I should get my hearing checked as well!'

Matt smiled, an all-encompassing smile that had Kelly's knees quivering. She sank down into her chair with relief. 'We're used to those types of everyday noises, but if you want, I could get my friend to give me a two-for-the-price-of-one deal.' One eyebrow rose mock-questioningly as he continued to smile down at her.

A real, genuine, full-blown smile from Matt Bentley. Why had she ever wanted one? It was dangerous. It was amazing. It was downright heart-stopping. His blue eyes lit up, the laughter lines around them creasing brightly. His even white teeth, which attested to braces in his youth, gleamed against his lower lip and his eyebrows took a break from being puckered into a frown.

Oh, he was a handsome man all right, and one who continued to do devastating things to her equilibrium. Say something, her brain demanded. Stop staring at him in a silly spaced-out way and say something. 'Er... Thanks...' She choked on her dry throat and cleared it quickly. 'Thanks anyway but I think I'll pass.'

'It's really no trouble, but I guess it's your choice.'

She returned his smile. 'Thanks for supporting me with what I had to say to Lorraine.'

'No problem. Thanks for asking me to join the fun.'

The intercom on her desk buzzed.

'Kelly, is Matt still in there?' Bianca's croaky voice came through.

'Is she all right?' Kelly asked Matt as he crossed to her desk. 'She's been coughing for the past two days.'

'Her asthma's playing up. Rhea's monitoring it.' Matt leaned over the opposite side of her desk and pressed the button. Kelly caught the scent of his aftershave and closed her eyes, savouring it.

'I'm here, Bianca.'

'Mr Mills is here.'

'Thanks. I'll be right out.'

She heard him straighten and slowly opened her eyes, only to find him looking intently down at her. 'You sure you're all right, Kelly?'

'Not when you're so close,' she found herself responding honestly.

Matt's gaze changed from one of concern to one of understanding. 'Ah.' He took a few steps away from her desk. 'Fair enough.'

'I meant that in a good way,' she clarified quickly.

'I know what you meant,' he replied with a nod, his earlier humour vanishing into thin air.

The intercom on her desk buzzed again. 'Attraction or no

attraction,' she said with a hint of valiance, 'the clinic must go on.'

He chuckled and nodded his agreement. 'See you.' He turned and walked calmly out of her room.

Kelly looked at the closed door then her intercom buzzed again. She quickly answered it, getting her mind off Matt Bentley and back on her work.

'This always worked well for me with morning sickness,' Rhea said as she pulled a green box of peppermint tea from a large basket she'd brought over and placed in the middle of the kitchen table. 'Have you got an infuser? The tea tastes much better when you use an infuser.' Rhea started rummaging around in her mother's kitchen drawers and Kelly just sat back and watched her. 'Also, I brought over some other essential items I thought you might need. Coconut oil and nipple cream.'

'Nipple cream?' Kelly reached into the basket and pulled the stuff out. 'Rhea, I'm only eight weeks gestation.'

Rhea straightened dramatically and placed her hands on her hips. 'Look, sunshine, I've been through this birth thing twice and now Joe's talking about having another one.'

'You don't want another one?'

'I don't mind,' Rhea said with a shrug, 'but you're missing the point, which is that pregnancy changes your body. You stretch in the most amazing way and when it's all over...' Rhea grabbed two handfuls of her stomach. 'Jelly-belly!'

'Jelly-belly?' Kelly laughed and rested a protective hand across her own flat stomach.

'Trust me, Kelly, it happens to most women. Your stomach sags and so do your breasts, and I'm not even going to touch on the subject of stretch marks.'

Kelly couldn't help it and gave way to her laughter. Rhea

joined in. 'You think I'm joking but I'm not. Ask any woman who's given birth. These things happen.'

'So cocoa butter and nipple cream are supposed to stop them?' Kelly picked up the products in question.

'No, but at least it will make you feel as though you still have some vestige of control over your body.' Rhea walked over to her side and placed a hand on her shoulder, the laughter fading from her eyes. 'I guess really what I'm trying to say is…enjoy it.'

'Oh, I intend to.' She smiled back up at the woman before her. She'd never really had a close female friend before but Rhea was rapidly penetrating Kelly's cocoon, making Kelly appreciate having another woman to talk to.

Perhaps it was her new maternal instinct shining through that was making her feel this way. Perhaps it was just hormones. She'd always prided herself on the fact that she'd never really needed anyone. Amazing how one tiny event— or person, she thought, giving her stomach an affectionate rub—could change her life for ever.

Rhea resumed her search for the infuser and crowed with triumph when she found it. She switched on the kettle. 'May as well make a brew now to see if you like it—or, rather, if the baby likes it.'

'Sure.'

Rhea busied herself with the cups. 'Have you told Matt yet?'

'What?' Kelly asked, deciding to play dumb.

'About the baby, of course.'

'No. Not yet. I wouldn't have told you if you hadn't guessed—not that I mean I wouldn't have told you at all, but just not so soon,' she added quickly.

'You're going to have to tell him sooner or later.'

'I know. I just need a little bit more time to get used to the idea myself. I only had it confirmed today.'

Rhea nodded and looked at Kelly. Her eyes were a lighter

blue than her brother's but now they held a hint of warning. 'Don't leave it too long,' she advised quietly. 'The longer you leave it, the harder it will be to tell him.'

Kelly nodded.

'You like my brother, don't you?' Rhea stated.

'Yes, I do.'

'What about the baby's father? Freddy, is it?'

'Yes. Freddy.' Kelly sighed and shook her head in shame. 'I feel so gullible.'

'What happened?'

'The night before we signed our divorce papers, Freddy took me out to dinner—you know, for old times' sake. It was then he told me he was having second thoughts. He said the year of our separation had been awful and we shouldn't go through with the divorce.'

'So it was messy?'

'No. That's just it. Freddy and I were friends, we still are. We spoke at least once a week during our separation and often met for lunch. We're friends.' Kelly shrugged. 'That's one of the reasons I wanted to end the marriage. The spark wasn't there any more. I was twenty-four when we married—far too young.'

'So what did you say when Freddy said he didn't want the divorce?'

'I was surprised but, then, that's Freddy. Always changing his mind at the last minute. He was so adamant, so sincere that I said I'd be willing to go to counselling to try and get back the spark we had. Anyway, one thing led to another and we ended up spending the night together. Our last night as husband and wife,' Kelly said wistfully.

She took the cup of tea Rhea offered and sniffed at it appreciatively. 'Thanks.'

'So in the morning he changed his mind?'

'Exactly. I was so cross with myself for believing him, for letting his fancy talk win me over. You'd think I'd have known him well enough to realise when he was spinning me a yarn.'

'Don't beat yourself up. We all make mistakes. So you both kept quiet and signed your papers.'

'Yes.' She sipped at the brew 'Mmm, this is nice.' She took another sip. 'I think the baby likes it.' She giggled a little as the alien words—'the baby'—rolled off her tongue so easily.

The front doorbell trilled and Kelly put her cup down. 'Excuse me.' She headed out of the kitchen and down the hallway to the door. 'Matt!' she said with surprise after she'd opened the door.

'Am I interrupting you?'

'No, no. Not at all.' She stood back as he opened the screen door. 'Please, come in.'

'Thanks. I…er…wanted to talk to you about Justin.'

'Sure. The kettle's just boiled. Would you like a tea or coffee?'

'Tea would be nice, thank you.'

'I'll get it,' Rhea called from the kitchen. 'You two go and sit down.'

'Sorry. I didn't know she was here.'

Kelly smiled at the awkward look which crossed his face. Didn't he want his sister to know he was calling on her? Even if it was under the guise of a medical discussion?

'I can go if you'd—'

'Matt,' she said calmly. 'It's fine. Come into the lounge room and sit down.' She led the way and sat in a comfortable armchair. 'You have some concerns about Justin?'

'Not concerns, but I've been thinking about things and just wanted to talk them through with you.' He settled onto the comfortable lounge. 'I checked a few of my books after the consult and came up with some other ideas as to what might be wrong with him. I think you're right to test for epilepsy and hearing, but if he passes both of those, the outcome could be substantially worse for Lorraine to deal with.'

Rhea walked into the lounge room carrying two cups, handing Kelly the one she'd been drinking and another one to Matt. 'I have to go,' she said. 'Joe's on night shift at the police station and will be leaving soon. I'll see you both tomorrow,' she threw over her shoulder as she turned and walked out of the room.

Kelly watched as Matt followed his sister's retreating back and then closed his eyes momentarily as though in pain. 'Something wrong?' she fished.

'Just that I'm going to get the third degree from Rhea to know the real reason I'm over here.'

'And what *is* the real reason?' Kelly shifted in her chair, curling her legs beneath her and being careful not to spill her tea. She sipped from the cup, her gaze never leaving his.

'Justin. I wanted to discuss Justin.'

'I don't doubt for one minute that you did but really, Matt, you don't need to be coy around me. If you wanted to come by just for a cup of tea and to chat, then by all means, please, do so. I like talking to you but for now let's get Justin out of the way. You were saying?'

Matt scratched his head as though he wasn't quite sure what to make of her. 'Coy? One thing I can tell you right now, Kelly is that I'm never *coy*. I may be quiet or thoughtful but never *coy*.'

Kelly laughed at his words and he joined in. 'Anyway, I did some reading today and there were a few other things we'll need to check for, Asperger's and autism being amongst them.'

'Well spotted.' She nodded encouragingly.

'You knew this?' he asked incredulously.

Kelly nodded. 'I wanted to take things slowly, hoping I wasn't right. I still do.'

'So I guess you've seen something like this before?'

She nodded again. 'Yes. We'll take things slowly with Lorraine and make sure she has whatever information and support she needs to get through it.'

'You're a fount of knowledge, Kelly O'Shea.' He sipped his tea. 'How long have you been travelling?'

Kelly rubbed one hand along the back of her neck, her fingers tangling in her curls. 'All my life, but as a doctor, it's been about six years now.'

'And you only do six-month locum stints?'

'Most of the time. Sometimes we used to take six months off and just ski or holiday somewhere quiet.'

'Sounds like the perfect marriage. What happened?'

Kelly sighed and shrugged, taking another drink from her cup. 'Stuff. No marriage could be perfect, I know that now. Freddy and I were far too immature and should never have married in the first place.'

'Bitterness?'

'No. It takes two to tango, as they say, and the decision to end our marriage was…sort of mutual.'

'Sort of?'

'We both wanted it to end but we had different reasons. All worked out for the best, though.' As she said the words, Kelly was immensely conscious of the baby inside her. It *had* worked out for the best, but what now?

'So you're…friends?'

'Yes.'

'Now, you see, I could never do that.'

'Do what?'

'Simply be friends with a woman I'd been married to.'

'You said you'd never been married.'

'No, I haven't, but that doesn't mean I don't know how I'd react.'

She exhaled slowly. 'I never meant to imply otherwise.'

Matt stood and started to pace around the room. Kelly

watched him carefully. The way his strong thighs pulled against the material of his trousers. The muscles that flexed in his arm as he raised his hand to rake his fingers through his hair. He was frustrated, uncomfortable and determined to make his point—and he'd never looked cuter.

Her gaze drifted to his butt but he turned and she quickly glanced up to meet his eyes.

'The woman I marry will be my soulmate—just like my parents. They've been married for almost forty years and they're still happy together.'

'So are my parents.'

'So how could you drift into such a loveless marriage?' He stood before her, his hands on his hips, almost accusing. Kelly frowned.

'It wasn't loveless, Matt, but it wasn't the kind of love soulmates share. We were both too young. Freddy was my best friend, we had so much in common and, well…' She shrugged. 'The rest, as they say, is history. People make mistakes, Matt.'

'You could have saved yourself so much heartache.'

'To tell the truth, I don't think I had any—heartache, that is.' She raised the cup to her lips the same time one of her legs started fizzing with pins and needles at being bent at such an odd angle for too long. 'Ah-h…' she spluttered as she shifted, spilling warm tea down her top and skirt. She shot out of the chair, resisting Matt's quickly outstretched hand, and put the cup on the table.

'Clumsy,' she said as she wiped her hand down her front, coughing a little from the way she'd swallowed the tea.

'Are you OK?' He patted her on the back. 'You didn't scald yourself?'

'No. No, I'm fine.' She smiled up at him, only then realising just how close they were. 'I guess I'm just too tired for my motor functions to work properly.'

Matt reached out and tucked a stray curl behind her ear.

'Hmm.' He gazed down into her eyes. 'You're beautiful,' he murmured as he shuffled his feet a bit closer. Their knees touched and Kelly drew in a breath, waiting in anticipation for the moment his lips would meet hers. '*Very* beautiful,' he corrected.

'Is this what you came here for?' she whispered.

'Must be.' He pressed a kiss to her cheek and her eyelids fluttered closed. 'I can't help it. I'm drawn to you, like a moth to the flame, and I'm not quite sure how to stop it.' A kiss on the other cheek.

'Then don't.' Kelly waited, not wanting to rush or push him. This had to be his decision, his choice. *But he doesn't have all the facts.* She quickly brushed the thought away. She only had a few more seconds to wait before his lips brushed tentatively against hers.

Her breath caught in her throat at the feather-light touch. It was wonderful. Tantalising and seductive. She wanted more—desperately—but this was Matt's call.

'Kelly.' He breathed her name and she opened her eyes, looking up into his gorgeous blue ones. 'This is so wrong.'

'Probably,' she whispered.

As though he was unable to control himself any longer, Matt slid his hands down her arms before lifting her hands to his shoulders. Kelly wasn't the type of person to look a gift horse in the mouth and eagerly wound her arms about his neck, her fingers plunging into the dark brown softness of his hair.

Matt rested his hands on her waist before closing his eyes at her touch. She gently massaged his scalp, waiting for his next move. *Tell him about the baby.* The internal warning kept playing over and over inside her mind while the agonising seconds ticked past. As soon as Matt kissed her, she knew all thought would disappear but...whatever happened between them next *had* to be his call.

'Mmm.' The sound was wrenched from him and she felt

his thumbs move in tiny circles against her waist. Then he started to tug on the material, pulling her half-wet shirt from the waistband of her skirt. His movements were slow yet steady and she realised he wasn't a man who liked to rush. He wanted to take his time and, although it was driving her insane with waiting, she couldn't deny the spark of potent sensuality that shot through her.

When his hands finally made contact with her back, he groaned and urged her closer. It was as though the skin-to-skin contact had thrown him over the edge. He pulled her roughly to him and brought his mouth down on hers, hard and urgent.

Although she was surprised, Kelly welcomed the change and met his passion head on. Their bodies seemed moulded to each other and she felt the cool moisture from the tea she'd spilt press against her skin. She should tell him the tea might stain his jumper, she should tell him she wasn't being fair to either of them. She should tell him about the baby. But all she could think about was the way his mouth felt on hers, the way he was making her feel and how his deep and sexy kisses were driving her insane.

She moaned in delight, deepening her response to his kiss. Never had she been kissed like this before, with such ardent desire, reaching a sense of fulfillment.

Her heart pumped wildly against her ribs and the sound reverberated through her ears. He felt so right…*so right*. Just this one kiss, she promised herself. Just this once. She'd been dreaming about how this might feel ever since she'd first laid eyes on him—and now she knew. It was… amazing. *He* was amazing. *They* were amazing.

'Mmm,' he groaned as he wrenched his mouth from hers, their breathing coming out in hard and fast gasps. His eyes were glazed but he smiled down at her, a little crooked smile that made her heart pound even faster. Had the man no idea how desirable he was?

He ran his tongue over his own lips. 'You taste like pep-permint.' His voice was husky, his blue depths dazed with passion. He kissed her forehead and her eyelids fluttered closed. He kissed them next, then the tip of her nose and finally…just when she thought he'd never get there…her mouth.

This time, though, he didn't linger long and she opened her eyes, an instant thread of anger bursting through her. How dared he deprive her of more of those delicious kisses? She felt a chuckle rumble from within him and frowned. The smile that creased his face was more potent than the one before and Kelly sighed with longing.

'You have very expressive eyes, Kelly,' he murmured as he pressed another quick kiss to her lips. 'Stunning, emerald-green eyes which scream of your impatience.' He chuckled. 'Your hair…' he took a handful of it and let the springy curls wind themselves around his fingers '…is beautiful. Your cheeks, your nose, your neck and your mouth…' He brushed a kiss across each as he spoke. 'All beautiful.'

When his mouth finally met hers again, Kelly melted. She clung to him and as he deepened the intensity, she felt her knees start to buckle and her head start to swim. She broke free and sighed. Never had a man made her feel so…precious. Never had a man made her feel faint!

She leant into him at the same time he shifted his feet and she felt herself start to lose her balance. Her eyes wid-ened in surprise as she glanced up at Matt, seeing a similar expression on his face as he shifted his stance again, trying to stop them from falling, but he was too late.

They overbalanced.

'Aagh,' Kelly yelled as she let go of Matt's head, her arms flailing around her sides, trying desperately to grab hold of something. The way they were standing, she would land first—with Matt coming down on top of her.

The baby! She had to protect the baby!

The urgent thought zoomed through her mind but it was all too late. Her knees continued to buckle and she crashed down, her bottom connecting with the carpeted floor first. Matt landed on top of her with a thud, knocking the air from her lungs.

She gasped and wriggled furiously to get him off her. 'Quick, Matt. Quick,' she said as she attempted to drag a breath in.

He started to shake and she wondered for a moment whether he'd hit his head or something on the way down. It took another moment to realise he was laughing.

'Matt, get off.'

His laughter died immediately at the concern in her voice.

'Quickly!' He was moving but it seemed to take for ever. 'Hurry, Matt, or you might hurt the baby.' The words of panic were out of her mouth before she could stop them, and when Matt finally sat on the floor beside her, all laughter was gone from his face.

'I beg your pardon? Did you say *baby*?'

CHAPTER FOUR

KELLY sighed and pushed her hair out of her eyes in dejected frustration. 'Yes. I'm pregnant.'

'What?' Matt didn't yell. He didn't roar. He merely sat there, the deepest frown taking up residence on his forehead, and he was looking at her as though she'd just grown an extra head.

'I'm eight weeks' gestation.'

He exhaled slowly and raked a hand through his hair. 'When did you find out?'

'I called up for the blood test results this morning.'

His jaw tightened. 'That pregnancy test I saw on your desk yesterday?'

'Mine.'

He nodded. 'That explains the peppermint tea and Rhea's visit. You'd better get her to check you out tomorrow, make sure you didn't do any permanent damage when we fell. I doubt it, but it's better to be safe than sorry. I presume, from your concern just now, that you're planning on keeping it?'

'Of course,' she replied with vehemence.

He was silent for a moment before asking, 'When were you going to tell me?'

Kelly looked down at her hands before meeting his gaze once more. 'Next week.' She wished he'd yell and scream at her. Get it out of his system, over and done with. This cool, professional façade was driving her crazy! 'Look, Matt, I didn't plan on—'

'Who's the father?' he interrupted.

'Freddy.'

He laughed without humour. 'A final goodbye?'

She shrugged, pushing away the hurtful memories of that evening. 'Something like that.'

'So what's next?'

'I don't know.'

He nodded and took a deep, steadying breath before getting up off the floor. He held out a hand to help her up but she waved it aside. 'I'm all right, thanks.'

They stood, staring at each other for a few uncomfortable moments. Kelly wanted to explain everything, to make him understand just how important this child was to her, yet at the same time it would be more baggage she was lumbering on him and that was one thing Kelly O'Shea never did. She never unloaded herself onto anyone. She would cope. She always had in the past.

'I should go.' Without waiting for her response, he turned and walked out of the room.

'Matt,' she called, going after him.

He rounded on her, holding up his hand for silence. 'Don't, Kelly. I don't want to know the intimate details but I do want you to think long and hard about what you're going to do for the next thirty-two weeks.' His voice was steely calm and she realised now that to have him yelling and screaming would have been taking the easy way out. Dealing with his calm professionalism was harder to bear because he was now treating her just like one of his patients. That in itself was worse than a slap across the face.

'You need to put the needs of your child first, and to start with I'd recommend a rethink on the motorbike. Where are you going to go in six months' time when this job ends? Another six-month position? Twelve months perhaps? Who's going to deliver the baby?' He picked up his coat and took a few steps towards the door. 'I gather you haven't told your ex-husband yet?'

She shook her head.

'More decisions.' He reached out and opened the door, a blast of cold winter air shooting into the house. It didn't make any difference to Kelly. Matt had already frozen her with his calm yet pointed questions. 'See you tomorrow.'

Tears welled up in her eyes the instant the door closed behind him. Silly. She was just being silly. She leant against the wall, burying her head in her hands as her shoulders started to shake. Why did his reaction leave her feeling this way? Guilty and devastated. It should be Freddy's reaction which concerned her—Freddy and his family and what they might do to her child.

The sobs racked her body and there seemed no way of stopping them. 'Hormones,' she grumbled out loud, giving the wall a little thump with her shoulder. Although, if she was at all honest about it, she shouldn't be blaming these tears on the hormones. It was because she'd let Matt down, and it made her feel horrible.

Matt sat in his chair and looked out at the bleak July evening. The sky was dark and cloudy—they'd get snow tomorrow. Good for the tourist trade.

Kelly was pregnant. The words floated around in his mind as he tried to grasp hold of the enormity of them. The woman he was attracted to was eight weeks pregnant. He slowly raised the glass of Scotch to his lips and took a sip.

He stood and unhooked the curtain, letting it fall and cover the bleakness outside, blocking it from view. If only he could do that with the feelings which were churning up inside him. How could she have kissed him like that when she was carrying another man's child?

He'd been fighting his feelings ever since she'd arrived, and tonight, when he'd lacked the self-control, he'd stupidly given in to them and she'd done nothing to stop him. *Nothing*. He'd been surprised when she hadn't taken the initiative after that first tentative kiss tonight, and now he knew why.

She'd wanted him to lead. That way, she could claim he had initiated the kiss, landing the responsibility of their actions squarely on his shoulders.

Kelly was good. Good at games of manipulation. No doubt she'd perfected them on her ex-husband, but he'd caught her out. He'd been able to read her body language and she'd been desperate for him to blow his top, to completely lose his cool so she could then calm him down and come out the victor.

Now, however, in the privacy of his own home, there was no need to fight his emotions. He could give his anger, disappointment and frustration full rein. He drained his glass and looked at it before giving into the impulse to smash it into the fireplace.

The sound of the crystal breaking was like music to his ears. Never had he done anything like that before and he was surprised at how satisfying it felt. It relieved a lot of his anger and frustration but his disappointment in Kelly remained.

'And it probably will,' he told himself. Then he turned and walked out of the room, leaving the mess behind him.

Kelly woke on Thursday morning knowing she'd have to face Matt again. She'd hardly slept and when she had, it had been because she'd cried herself to sleep.

She sat up and took a sip of water from the bottle she kept by her bed. Moments later, she was running for the bathroom, her hand clamped firmly over her mouth. When it was over, she shuffled into the kitchen, pulling the ends of the cord to her dressing-gown together, her feet snug and warm inside her sheepskin-lined slippers. She boiled the kettle, intent on drinking a cup of the peppermint tea to see if it really did help the nausea she was experiencing.

The cups she'd brought in from the front room late last night still sat on the draining-board, waiting to be washed.

It was a gentle reminder of what had transpired with Matt and she didn't need it. She could remember it all quite clearly. Those wonderful kisses followed by utter withdrawal, physically and mentally.

It was the way he'd looked at her—as though she were just another interesting specimen in a Petri dish in a lab. She'd realised this was Matt's way of dealing with things, but as she'd been so used to Freddy and his often explosive temper, she'd been thrown off guard when Matt hadn't reacted in the same way. Although why she'd expected it she wasn't sure. Matt was nothing like Freddy. Quite the opposite, in fact.

The kettle boiled and she made herself some tea, sipping it slowly whilst nibbling on a dry cracker. Within a few minutes, she was feeling decidedly better and silently praised Rhea for her assistance in the matter.

There was no way she'd be able to avoid Matt today, not with Justin's EEG scheduled for nine o'clock. Speaking of which, if she didn't get a move on, she'd be late. Not the best way to start getting back into Matt's good books. She'd been amazed to find his opinion, whether it was good or bad, was extremely important to her. Therefore, naturally, she wanted it to be good.

She arrived at the hospital and set the EEG machine up. There was a special hat which they'd need to put on Justin's scalp and she wondered how she was going to get him to stay still long enough for them to get a good reading.

Thankfully, Lorraine turned up with his favourite toys, drinks and food.

'You're a smart woman,' Kelly said.

'Where's Matt?' Lorraine asked.

'Uh…I'm not sure. I was just thinking the same thing. I'll give the clinic a buzz. Maybe he's been held up.' As she headed to the phone, he burst through the door and Kelly stopped in mid-stride. The way his hair was mussed by the wind, the way his eyes were as bright as the sky on a summer's day, the way his lips smiled in a greeting to Lorraine—everything about him stopped her. He looked good enough to eat.

Kelly's shoulders shook involuntarily as a shiver of awareness coursed down her spine. Her heart did a somersault when he turned and looked at her, his gaze sweeping quickly over her neat trousers, tailored shirt and matching bustier vest. He lingered a moment too long on where she would soon be growing larger before meeting her gaze.

'Sorry I'm late.' He took off his thick coat and scarf. 'I decided a brisk walk was in order this morning but I got stopped by people along the way. Bad move.'

His deep tone washed over her and she found herself smiling up at him. She reached out and removed a twig from his hair. 'You won't be needing this.' She twirled it between her fingers.

'Er…thanks.' Matt couldn't understand it. How could his body still respond so quickly to her when he knew she was pregnant? That shouldn't be possible. He'd spent the night talking sternly to himself about his attraction to Kelly, telling himself that whatever he felt for her had to be put into stasis. Still, one look at her had his body reacting, and all of the previous night's mental therapy was wiped away.

He turned and hung his coat and scarf up, hoping for a few seconds to calm his racing thoughts. Thoughts which had nothing to do with the patient before him but everything to do with his colleague.

He needed self-control and he now wondered where on earth he was supposed to find it. She looked very business-like in her tailored navy pinstripe suit. Perhaps it was the bustier she was wearing. He'd never seen anything like it in his life, and just the way it was moulded to her breasts was almost enough to make him hyperventilate.

She was pregnant! If he kept repeating that to himself

often enough, hopefully it would help him maintain some sort of self-control. He raked his hair back into place with one hand, ignoring the tingling sensation of where Kelly's fingers had briefly touched him.

'Shall we begin?' she asked, and he nodded. 'Lorraine has brought in Justin's favourite toys as well as some food and drink. I think we should use the food as a last resort and try the toys and drink first as methods of distraction.'

'Sure.' Matt smiled at Lorraine. 'He'll get upset—any child would, and I don't blame him. He'll be confused, not understanding what's going on, and he'll be looking to you for reassurance and support.'

Lorraine bit her lip and nodded. 'OK.'

'Right, then. Lorraine, if you could come and sit here in this comfortable chair and hold Justin quite firmly on your lap. Keep his arms down by his sides because his first reaction will be to try and rip everything off.'

'OK.' Lorraine did as she was asked and Kelly got Matt to help her as they put the special EEG cap onto Justin's head. As she'd suspected, he squirmed and squealed and started to cry. Kelly's heart turned over with anguish for him and she, along with Matt, did everything they could to help Lorraine cope.

'He's a strong little thing,' Matt responded five minutes later as Justin continued to thrash around and scream.

'How about a bottle, Lorraine?' Kelly suggested. The toy car hadn't worked its usual magic, even when Lorraine had spun the wheels.

He rejected the bottle but Matt urged her to try again. She did, and this time Justin reluctantly took it. It was enough to keep him still and that was one thing they needed from him—to be completely still.

When the bottle was finished, he seemed to have grudgingly accepted the 'thing' on his head and was happy to spin the wheels on his toy car.

After twenty minutes, Kelly came and removed the par-
aphernalia from him, telling him what a good boy he'd been.
She checked with Lorraine before pulling a lollypop out of
her trouser pocket and giving it to Justin.

'So, how long until you know the results?' Lorraine
asked.

'We know them now. His brain patterns and functions are
fine,' Kelly answered.

'Does that mean no epilepsy?'

'Correct.'

Lorraine sagged with relief. 'Whew! I hardly slept a wink
last night.'

'You poor thing.' Kelly could quite easily sympathise as
she'd hardly slept herself, but for a completely different
reason.

'Hearing test next?'

'That's right.' Both women turned to look at Matt who
nodded.

'Right. I've contacted a Dr Natasha Forest at Wangaratta
hospital. She works in the A and E department and has set
up a hearing test for Justin for Monday morning. Are you
able to get there on Monday morning?' he asked Lorraine.

'So long as it's not too early.'

'Ten o'clock.' Matt walked over to his coat and pulled
out a piece of paper.

She nodded. 'That should be fine, but why do we have
to go to A&E?'

'You don't have to go into the treatment area, that's just
where Natasha works. Ask for her and she'll take good care
of you. You know, show you where the audio testing room
is and where the cafeteria is—that sort of thing. I thought
it might make you feel less alone.'

'So she's a friend of yours?' Lorraine asked as she studied
the information.

'A good and trusted friend.' He said the words earnestly

and Kelly felt a hint of annoyance at the unknown Natasha
for being held high in Matt's esteem. 'As neither Kelly nor
I would be able to be there with you, I gave Natasha a call
and asked if she wouldn't mind being a proxy. She's a
lovely woman. You'll like her.'

'If you say so.'

'I do and now, as Justin's had a stressful morning, why
don't you take him home and see if he'll have a little sleep?'

'Ha. Wishful thinking.' Lorraine gathered everything up
and, taking Justin by the hand, headed towards the door.
'Thanks—both of you. Come on, Justin. Home time.'

'You're welcome,' Kelly and Matt said in unison. Matt
held the door for her and the instant it closed, he turned to
look at Kelly.

'That went quite well.'

'Yes.' Kelly busied herself, packing away the equipment.
'I was quite proud of Justin and the way he coped.'

'Do you still think it might be autism?' he asked.

'Well, some form of autism. There are several different
levels. We need to know what resources the Autism
Association provides.'

'Preparing for a worst-case scenario?'

'I don't know. I wouldn't call it *worst* case but probably
not what Lorraine was expecting when she came to the doctor so we could help her son get some sleep.'

'True.'

'Our job is to provide guidance and support for Lorraine
during this time. Just like you did with your friend Natasha.
That was a nice touch, Matt.'

He nodded. 'I thought it might help Lorraine feel more
comfortable and Natasha is a great person.'

His eyes lit up when he spoke about her and Kelly had a
burning urge to know more about this woman. How important was she to Matt? 'I presume you've known her a long
time? Grew up together?'

'No. Actually, she's only been in this part of the country for about three years.' He looked down at his hands. 'Her husband was a good friend of mine.'

Kelly picked up on the past tense. 'What happened?'

'He died in a car accident six months after they were married. That was over two years ago now.'

'Oh, Matt.' Kelly walked over and placed her hand on his shoulder.

'It's Natasha my sympathy goes out to. Conrad was her second husband and now he's dead as well. Widowed twice and she's just turned twenty-nine.'

Kelly sucked in a deep breath. 'The poor woman.' She dropped her hand back to her side but Matt reached out and took it in his.

'She's a very strong woman. I've been surprised by her inner strength since the accident, although her daughter Lily probably has something to do with that.'

'How old is Lily?'

'She's six and is from Natasha's first marriage.' Matt turned Kelly's hand over in his and looked down at their entwined fingers. 'Conrad was sterile due to a radiation accident when he was a child so it was nice when he married Natasha and had an instant family. He adored Lily. Loved her like his own.'

Kelly nodded. 'I can understand that.' She bit her lower lip nervously, knowing now was the perfect time to confide in Matt. 'I was told I'd never have children either.'

Matt's fingers tightened at her words. 'What?'

'I have endometriosis, Matt. Freddy had a low sperm count.' She shrugged. 'We never used contraception, there was no need.'

'How bad is the endometriosis?'

'Enough that I need to have D and Cs regularly.'

He was silent for a moment, absorbing the information

and gazing down into her eyes. 'And now you're pregnant.' He spoke the words softly. 'A miracle.'

Tears blurred her vision and she nodded. 'Yes.' She felt her heart pound more fiercely against her ribs as they simply stood there, staring into each other's eyes. They were connecting. Really connecting. Not just their minds but their souls as well.

She felt a gentle tug on her hand, urging her closer. Matt leaned down and placed a quick kiss on her cheek before breaking all contact and taking a few steps back.

'I need to go.'

'Matt, wait. Can't we talk about this?'

'What is there to talk about, Kelly?' He didn't raise his voice.

'This…attraction we feel.'

'What about it?'

She stared at him—amazed. 'Matt…it's…incredible. You make me feel so…cherished and beautiful and needed. I've never felt this way before.'

Those words told him a lot about her marriage. 'Maybe it's the hormones making you feel this way. They're usually heightened during pregnancy.'

'It's not the hormones,' she stated crossly.

'How do you know? The entire time you've been here you've been pregnant, even if you didn't know about it.' His tone was clear and concise.

Matter-of-fact-Matt! It was enough to send her taut emotions over the edge.

'Will you stop speaking to me in that ''doctor'' tone? I am not your patient, Matt, and neither do I want to be.'

'What *do* you want from me, Kelly?' He didn't rise to her bait but kept his voice at its usual level.

She waved her arms about in the air as though trying to grab hold of a label that fitted their circumstances, but came up empty. 'I don't know but that's what I want to find out.'

He looked at her and shook his head. 'You have a lot of issues in your life right now, Kelly, and you don't need me as an added complication.'

'Maybe I don't consider you a complication.'

'Well, I do. You need to sort things out and the last thing you should be doing is starting something up with me. I don't need the aggravation and neither do you. In eight months' time, give or take a few weeks, you'll be giving birth. You'll need to find a job when this one finishes, somewhere to stay, a doctor to deliver your child and, of course, tell your ex-husband he's going to be a father.' He ground out the last words and it was the first bit of real emotion he'd displayed. 'Anything between us, other than as colleagues, would be futile.'

She could see his point. Quite clearly, in fact. It was the logical thing to do and she'd realised within minutes of her initial meeting with Matt that he was a man who thrived on logic. The problem was, being logical wasn't always right.

Still, he was communicating with her, which was a miracle in itself considering his gender. She should be grateful for it and she was, even if she disagreed with him. If he wanted everything to be done in a clear, calm and orderly fashion, she would do just that.

'I see your point, Matt, and thank you for expressing your concern and opinion—an opinion, I might add, which I value. Even though we've only known each other a short time, I feel as though it's been a lot longer.'

'Agreed.'

'I'll address your concerns and keep my professional distance on one condition.'

He eyed her warily. 'What?'

'You kiss me goodbye.'

'I just did.'

'You call that a goodbye kiss? No way, mate. I want a

proper humdinger of a kiss goodbye. After all, it has to last me until I can talk you into a repeat.'

He shook his head. 'No repeats Kelly.'

'Then you'd better make it a good one,' she whispered seductively.

Matt raked his hand through his hair, ruffling it just the way she liked it. She smiled up at him, waiting.

'All right,' he said eventually. 'One goodbye kiss.'

Kelly's smile increased as she took a step closer, almost daring him to back away. He stood his ground, his gaze flicking between her eyes and her lips. If he was waiting for her to make the first move, wanting her to start the ball rolling, she was more than happy to.

She reached out and placed her hands at his waist, bringing their bodies into contact. Taking her time, she opened her palms out flat, moving them around to the front of his chest. She closed her eyes, committing every solid millimetre of him to memory. The feel of him beneath her hands was electrifying and she felt the buzz pass from him up her arms and into her body.

His crisp, white work shirt was cool to her touch and she raised her hands to his shoulders, sliding them beneath his suit jacket and pushing it off. He moved his arms slightly, and within the next instant his jacket fell to the floor. Matt didn't move, simply let her touch him.

Kelly's impatience sparked to life and she worked hard to control it. She moved her hands around to his back, feeling his ribs and muscles beneath her fingers. Needing more, she decided to take a page out of his book and gently tugged at the material at his waistband.

When her hands finally made contact with his skin, she parted her lips, allowing the pent-up breath to escape. Matt seemed to reciprocate her feelings as he closed his eyes and groaned with delight. Her fingers retraced their steps, coming around to the front of his body, feeling the warmth of his skin and relishing in it.

Perfume, aftershave, hospital disinfectant and natural pheromones made a heady mixture and one that fuelled her desire for him. Matt arched his head back, his breathing deep and erratic. Kelly reached up a little and pressed her lips to his Adam's apple, glad that her shoes gave her the extra height.

It appeared Matt was enjoying this goodbye kiss and she couldn't resist the urge to tease him a little. Carefully, she moved her hands slowly downwards, delighting once again in the firmness of his washboard stomach. He was obviously a man who took a great care of himself.

When her fingers came to rest on the buckle of his belt, Matt's head snapped forward, his eyes opened and his free hand came to rest on hers, stilling her fingers. Kelly laughed up at him and it was then he saw the teasing glint in her eyes.

She wanted to play, eh? Well, he'd certainly join in the game. Bringing his mouth into contact with hers, he nipped at her lower lip before slowly running his tongue around the circumference of her mouth. Her hands had moved back around to his back, bringing their bodies into contact. Matt pressed his mouth to hers again and this time moved firmly over it, his tongue seeking out a response and welcoming the one she offered.

His hands rested at her waist, his thumbs just touching the lower part of her breasts. The pinstriped bustier and the way it clung perfectly to her shape had been driving him insane since he'd first walked through the door.

He moved his hand up slightly, his finger still moving in tiny circles, and when she gasped against his mouth Matt felt his resolve begin to snap. He knew if he wasn't careful, this goodbye kiss might end up being more than just a kiss. He had to keep control. It was imperative, yet Kelly had already shown she could make him lose complete control, regardless of his resolve.

His fingers continued to move up, lightly tantalising her breasts through the fabric to where a column of white buttons sat at the base of her neck. Pressing his mouth to hers in a renewal of his desire for her, Matt worked the top three buttons open. Her hands, on his back, were urging him closer and he knew she needed to feel their torsos melded together—but he had other plans.

His fingers pushed her collar and the open part of her shirt apart at the same time his mouth left hers to trail a path of hot fiery kisses across her cheek, his teeth momentarily nipping at her earlobe before continuing on down her neck towards the valley of her breasts.

Kelly gasped and threw her head back, unable to believe how much this man affected her. Inside, her body was burning up as a fever of utter pleasure exploded once again and her stomach seemed alive with churning butterflies. Nothing existed beyond this moment in time. Nothing existed but the two of them.

She lightly scratched her nails down his back, feeling him arch slightly. She was desperate for his mouth to return to hers yet at the same time she didn't want him to stop the sweet spread of kisses he continued to place lovingly on her body.

With an agonising intensity, Matt knew if he didn't do something about stopping soon, he wouldn't have the willpower or strength to do so. Would Kelly stop him? Would she let them go too far? He didn't know. It reinforced just how little he knew about this woman who affected him so completely. He raised his head to claim her lips once more and started to slow things down.

She knew what he was doing and didn't try to stop him. She knew this kiss couldn't possibly be the end for them but… Wow! If this was the beginning, she couldn't wait to see what the next episode had in store for them, but as far as Matt was concerned, this was it—goodbye.

Easing off slowly, he eventually withdrew his mouth from hers, pulling her close and resting her head on his chest. The sound of his erratically pounding heart mimicked her own and she held him for as long as she could.

She wasn't quite sure how long they stood there, content to hold each other, but by the time Matt took a step back, relinquishing his hold on her, their heartbeats had returned to normal.

He bent and picked up his jacket, shrugging into it before reaching for his thick winter coat. He put it on and hooked his scarf around his neck, buttoning the coat closed, hiding his untucked shirt.

Their gazes met and held and he slowly brought one hand up to cup her cheek. 'You're a wonderful person, Kelly. Thanks for sharing a part of yourself with me.' He dropped his hand and stepped towards the door. 'Goodbye.' And then he left.

CHAPTER FIVE

MATT shifted his goggles and placed his stocks in the snow, getting ready to move off. Here, in the brilliant whiteness of winter, treading along the cross-country track, he felt at peace. He took a deep breath and started to move, glad to be doing something physical at last.

He'd hardly slept for the past two nights—last night having been the worst. He'd ended up prowling agitatedly around his house during the wee small hours, finally deciding to concentrate on paperwork. He'd sat in his study and, unable to get his mind to work properly, had shifted back the curtain to gaze out into the blackness of night.

The window of his parents' house which had faced him was the room Kelly was sleeping in, and when he'd seen the light suddenly peek out from the edge of the curtains, he'd become instantly alert.

Was she being sick? Was she all right? Perhaps she'd skipped dinner and needed a snack. She shouldn't be skipping her meals, she should be making sure the baby had enough sustenance to grow strong and healthy.

Was she lying in bed reading a book or wandering around the house like himself? He wanted to go over and see if she was all right because he'd hate something bad to happen to her, especially as she was all alone. He even returned to his room and started pulling on his jeans before stopping, realising he'd have to explain his presence. He took the jeans off and hung them back up in the closet.

Groaning, he went back to bed. Kelly O'Shea was driving him insane. He decided the only way to get his mind off her was by reading the new information he'd collected on autism. He woke with the thick text draped over his chest, his head at an odd angle against the headboard.

Now, thank goodness, he was surrounded by an environment he loved, with the sound of snow crunching beneath his skis. The briskness of the day was all around him and the exercise he was planning on doing should definitely help him sleep tonight.

Kelly was doing the Saturday morning clinic and Rhea was working at the Yankandandah hospital, which was one of the three hospitals in their co-op. With no females to bother him, he was determined to enjoy his day off—pushing Kelly and that mind-shattering kiss they'd shared out of his thoughts.

Matt made his way along the track and back to the ski lodge in time for a late lunch. Mt Buffalo was outdoing herself today—it was glorious. Perfect skiing weather. He was greeted by Jana, who was waitressing at the café, and waited for the usual pangs of uneasiness to engulf him. Nothing happened. He frowned, wondering why she didn't affect him the way she always had since high school.

'Hi, Matt,' Jana crooned, and ran a red-tipped finger nail across the shoulders of his ski-suit. 'Lookin' good.'

'Thanks, Jana.' Usually he'd feel a pang of regret if she touched him like that but today—nothing. 'How's everything with you?'

'Pretty bad.' She pushed her fingers into her spiky red hair, making it stand on end even more. 'I'm thinking of leaving the mountain and going to Melbourne.' Matt laughed and Jana hit his arm. 'What's so funny?' she asked hotly.

'You've been saying that for years and you never do. This mountain is in your blood and you've been to Melbourne several times. If you want to go somewhere different, try going overseas.'

'Trying to get rid of me, Matt?' Her tone was inquisitive.

'No.' Matt shook his head, his lips still twitching with amusement. He was amazed at how free he felt in her presence. In fact, he was hard pressed to remember what had initially attracted him to her in the first place. She had no direction, no sense of adventure, no…spirit!

Unlike Kelly. The thought struck him suddenly and he realised the truth in it.

'Jana…' He took her elbow in his hand and lead her over to a quiet table. 'Sit down for a second. One of the reasons we broke up was because you'd never take a chance. You talked of leaving so many times but you never followed through.'

'I know, I know. I remember. You told me at the time I needed more direction in my life and that you weren't going to wait around while I blew hot and then cold.'

'Sounds as though you remember it word for word.'

'So?'

He smiled. 'That was five years ago, Jana.'

'So? It had a big impact on me. You'd been following me around since high school, Matt, and I know my ''bad girl'' image was what attracted you in the first place. But…' she sighed. 'High school was a long time ago and I'm still not sure who I am.'

Matt placed his hand on hers. 'Keep searching, because you're the only one who can find out.'

Jana looked down at their hands and Matt quickly removed his. She angled her head. 'You're different.'

Matt laughed. 'Why? Because you and I are having a civil conversation?'

'You were always civil, Matt. It was one of things that drove me mad about you. You're always calm, always logical.'

He shrugged nonchalantly. 'All I can tell you, Jana, is to do whatever makes you happy. If you want to leave the mountain then give it serious consideration. Look at it logically.'

'Is that what you're doing? Are you happy, Matt?'

He looked into her blue eyes and was amazed when nothing happened. He'd *always* had an emotional response to Jana, even when Louise had come into the picture, but now…nothing. His stomach growled saving him from answering her question.

'Is it too late to get lunch?'

'We have stopped serving but I can see what the chef can do for you.' She stood. 'Thanks, Matt.'

'For what?'

She shrugged. 'For being my friend.' With that she headed off into the kitchen. Matt settled back in the chair and soon Jana came out with a plateful of pasta. 'Your favourite,' she said. 'I'm going on my break now so enjoy it.'

Matt did, feeling as though a huge weight had been taken off his shoulders. He and Jana had finally made it to the 'friends' category after a relationship. It had certainly taken them long enough. It made him think of his comment to Kelly that he could never be friends with a woman he'd been married to. Well, he hadn't been married to Jana but he'd been close to proposing several times, although something had always held him back.

Was this how Kelly felt about her ex-husband? Did they have this kind of friendship? His thoughts were cut short as several people stopped by to say hello. Some were patients, some were friends, some were both. The time passed easily enough and after paying his bill and waiting one hour after he'd eaten, Matt walked back to his car and grabbed his alpine skis before heading out to the slopes.

The tourists were out in droves today, which was good for the economy as Bright and the surrounding districts relied heavily on the tourist trade. He perched on the chairlift which took him to the top of the hill, watching as some children made their way down with one of the ski-school instructors.

At the top, he adjusted his goggles and started on his way down the slope. He felt invigorated and his recent tension slowly started to fade. The white landscape was dotted with people wearing colourful ski-suits, and as he headed back to the chair-lift he watched a woman in a black and red suit make her way to the bottom. Her technique was faultless, as was her figure, even beneath the bulk of the suit, and…she was skiing straight towards him.

She swerved to a stop, spraying snow over his legs. Planting her stocks firmly into the ground, she lifted her goggles off and ripped off her black beanie. Red curls cascaded down and bounced around her shoulders.

'Howdy, pardner,' Kelly said, imitating a cowboy.

'What are you doing here?' he spluttered, completely taken by surprise. His gut twisted with the knowledge that he'd been attracted to her even before he'd found out it was her in that sleek, colourful ski-suit.

'I'm skiing, silly.' Kelly laughed up at him, glad she'd surprised him.

'What about the clinic?'

She shrugged. 'No one was booked in so I shut up shop.'

'Kelly! What if a call comes in?'

'Oh, surely they can wait until one of us decides to return.'

'Kelly!' His tone was incredulous. One thing he despised was people who didn't take their commitments seriously. He demanded one hundred per cent all the time. If Kelly thought she could get away with behaviour like this, she was sadly mistaken.

'Matt!' She laughed again. 'I'm joking. You do realise what the time is, don't you?'

He shoved one stock into the ground and went to take

off his glove so he could get beneath his sleeve to find out what the time was.

'Don't bother.' She laughed, reaching out a red-gloved hand to stop him. 'It's a quarter to four. I saw the last patient just after two o'clock—we were busy,' she added. 'Then I left Bianca to lock up the surgery—as she always does—grabbed my ski stuff and came up the mountain.'

'On your motorbike! Kelly, you could have lost control on any of those winding bends—'

'I've leased a car, Matt,' she interrupted.

'And had an accident and miscarried,' he finished. Then her words sank in. 'You've leased a car?'

'Sure. I swapped it for the bike.'

He frowned. 'Good. Good. I'm glad about that. Very sensible of you but just make sure you take it easy on the slopes.'

'Why?' It was her turn to frown.

'Because you're *pregnant*.'

'Oh, Matt.' She laughed. 'You really take the cake in the over-protective stakes. The baby's about the size of a peanut at the moment.'

'It's no laughing matter. You could miscarry.'

'I could miscarry walking down the street.' She brushed the suggestion away. 'I'm not going to live my life that way, always asking "what if".'

'At least take note of the statistics. Endometriosis sufferers are more inclined to miscarry—'

'*Any* pregnancy could miscarry. I know I need to take it easier as the pregnancy progresses but, seriously, right now? The baby is well shielded. Besides…' she bent and picked up a handful of the powdery white stuff '…this is snow.' She balled it in her gloved hands and tossed it at him. It hit his shoulder. 'It's soft.'

'Kelly,' he warned.

'All right, Matt. I'll be careful,' she promised, knowing

she wasn't going to get him off the topic until she did so. 'I'm an experienced skier who has skied worse slopes than this one. In fact…' Kelly turned and looked at the slope in question '…I don't know if we can even call this a "slope". It's more like a gentle incline.'

'Yes, but you weren't pregnant when you skied the other death-defying slopes.' He looked down at her and shook his head. 'I guess as the sun will soon be setting I'd better keep you company. At least that way I'll know you're really looking after yourself.'

Kelly smiled sweetly up at him. 'Now, how could a girl say no to that? If it wasn't against the rules, I'd kiss you, Matt Bentley.'

His Adam's apple worked overtime as he swallowed. 'Just as well it's against the rules, then.'

She laughed, feeling as giddy as a schoolgirl while she tucked her hair back into her beanie, put her goggles back on and pulled on her gloves, noticing his gaze was transfixed on every move she made. She pulled her stocks free and together they headed over to the chair-lift.

They had about an hour and a half more daylight and used every second. Matt was charming and considerate, as well as a little over-protective. Usually, she would get annoyed with people who watched over her in the way he did, but instead she found it reassuring. Could it be the hormones? Or was it simply Matt?

As she headed off down the slope again, she reflected on how totally different he was from Freddy. She'd once thought Freddy was the man of her dreams but somewhere along the line that dream had changed. Matt, however, managed to make her sizzle deep down inside with one simple, smouldering look. His mind might be telling him that starting something up with her was a bad move, but his body was obviously telling him the exact opposite.

Every time she'd mentioned Freddy, Matt had grimaced.

Even when he'd said the words 'ex-husband' the other day, she'd noted that same thread of annoyance and disgust in his tone. Did that mean he was jealous of Freddy? Jealous of the man who had been her husband and was the father of her unborn child? If he was, she was definitely doing something right!

If Matt was jealous, it meant he had strong feelings for her, and it was that hope which kept Kelly's resolve intact. She would deal with everything he wanted and when she knew the answers to the questions he'd asked, she intended to see where this attraction, which had sprung from nowhere, ended up.

At the end of the run, Matt stopped and waited for her to come down. 'It's starting to get dark and those blue-grey clouds look as though they're bringing more snow.'

'Is the café still open?' she asked. 'I could do with a cup of coffee.'

'Sure, but you can't drink coffee any more. How about herbal tea? I'll see if they've got peppermint.'

Kelly smiled. 'That would be lovely.' Matt attached her skis to the roof-rack on her car while she protested. 'I'm more than capable, Matt.'

'The problem with you, Kelly O'Shea, is that when people offer to help you out, you think they're implying you're not capable.'

'Aren't they?'

'Not necessarily.' He worked quickly and efficiently and she could tell he'd done the job a hundred times before. 'I was simply being a gentleman and doing something nice for you. Not only that, I'd do it for any other person if they asked—male or female.'

'But I didn't ask.'

He smiled down at her. 'You don't need to ask. I'm more than happy to volunteer.'

Kelly's heart did a flip-flop at the look he gave her. His

blue eyes radiated happiness and for that split second she knew she felt the same way. 'So, does that mean you'll let me help you get your skis onto your car?'

'Sure, but I've just noticed that quite a few people are heading into the lodge so why don't you go grab us a couple of chairs and I'll be in once I'm finished?'

'I know what you're up to, mate.' She waggled her finger playfully at him. 'And I'll let you get away with it, but only this once. Understand?'

'Yes, Doctor,' he replied.

Kelly went inside, realising Matt was right. Most of the tables were full of people ripping off gloves and hats and unzipping ski-suits, laughing and joking after having fun in the snow. It was an atmosphere she loved and here she was—about to share it with Matt.

She sat down at a table and took off her gloves. The waitress, whose name tag identified her as Jana, came over to take her order. Kelly wasn't sure whether Matt wanted tea or coffee but decided, as he'd sent her inside, he'd get stuck with whatever she ordered.

She pulled off her beanie and Jana gasped at her hair. 'Nice curls. Are they natural?'

Kelly smiled. It wasn't the first time she'd had comments on her hair. People with straight hair often envied her curls while Kelly, naturally, wanted her hair to curl a little less tightly. 'Yes.'

'They're gorgeous.'

'Thanks.' She spotted Matt coming in the door and waved. Matt saw her and headed in her direction.

'Hi, Jana.' He sat down opposite Kelly.

'Do you have any yummy cheese cakes, pastries or strudels on offer?' Kelly asked Jana. The waitress looked from her to Matt and back again before nodding slightly.

'What about apple strudel?' Matt asked.

'Huh? Oh, sure. The apple strudel is delicious.'

'Then we'll have two,' Kelly said decisively. 'And two herbal teas, please.'

'Tell me if they compare to the ones you've had in Austria.'

'What, the tea?'

'No.' He laughed. 'The strudel.'

'Oh. How did you know I'd been to Austria?' Kelly asked.

He smiled and her heart reacted the way it usually did. 'I didn't. Just a guess.'

Kelly turned to look at Jana who was still standing beside their table, her pen poised on the notepad. The body language from the other woman was one of intrigue and Kelly was surprised she hadn't picked up on it the instant Matt had sat down.

'I take it you two know each other?' she said, bringing her thoughts into the open.

'That's right.' Matt nodded, feeling a little uncomfortable at Kelly's directness. 'Jana and I have known each other since high school.'

Kelly noted the way Matt shifted in his chair. Her question had clearly struck a mark and she instinctively knew there was more to it than he was letting on. 'So you used to date, eh?'

'Yes.' He glanced up at Jana before looking back to Kelly. 'But that was a long time ago.'

'I'll…um…just go put…your order in,' Jana said uncomfortably before heading off.

Matt shook his head but there was a twinkle in his eyes. 'What?'

'You shouldn't be so open and forthright, Kelly. This is sleepy, relaxing snow country where people aren't used to such straightforwardness.'

Kelly laughed. 'Thanks for the tip. I'll try to remember that.' A pain in her stomach made her groan and she shifted.

'What's wrong?' Matt was instantly alert.

'Just hunger. I'm finding I need to eat more frequently rather than just three meals a day.'

'Eating for two, eh?' He relaxed back in his chair.

'No. I'm hungry, that's all. Besides, I'm going to have to be more careful about what I eat from now on.'

'Listeriosis,' he said with a nod.

'Gotta keep that infectious organism away from my baby.'

'Don't go overboard, though. You still need to eat a healthy diet.'

'Yes, Doctor.' She nodded seriously.

'And it's only for the first trimester. The organism is usually only found in foods that haven't been prepared properly. That's why I suggested the apple strudel instead of the cheese cake—not that I'm saying the foods aren't prepared well here, they are, but soft cheeses are known to be carriers of the organism.'

'Good call,' she agreed. 'Besides, I'm a sucker for apple strudel, especially if it's made the Austrian way. My mother was taught how to make it when we lived in Salzburg.'

Matt was intrigued. It was the first voluntary mention of her family. 'How old were you then?'

She frowned. 'About nine. We moved to Vienna when I was ten and then to London when I was eleven. I don't remember having two birthdays in one place.' She shrugged.

'How many languages do you speak?'

'Eight, if you don't count a lot of the African dialects I picked up.'

'Quite the linguist.'

Kelly shrugged again and sat back in her chair when she spotted Jana headed in their direction. 'Thanks.' Kelly smiled up at her. Matt pulled the zipper down on his ski-suit and dug inside, pulling out his wallet. 'Oh, no,' Kelly responded, scrambling for her own purse. 'This is my treat.'

'I've got it,' he told Kelly.

She reached out over the table, putting her hand onto his, stopping him. 'Please, Matt.' Their gazes held for a moment and he reluctantly put his wallet away.

'That's a first,' Jana remarked. 'Matt's always been big on playing the chivalrous male.'

'Times change.' Matt shrugged.

Kelly handed the money to Jana. 'The strudel looks magnificent!' And Kelly dug right in. 'Mmm.' She swallowed. 'Tastes magnificent, too.'

'Glad you enjoy it,' Jana replied, before leaving.

Matt chuckled. 'That's a huge compliment, coming from you. I'll have to remember to tell the chef.'

'Let me guess, you went to school with him, too?'

'As a matter of fact, I did.' Matt followed suit and started to eat his strudel.

'I find it quite interesting that you've probably known most of the locals in this room since pre-school.'

'Either that or they've known me since then, but there are also a lot of tourists here and they certainly don't know me.' He added one sugar to his tea, stirred it and took a sip. Kelly was surprised at how excited she felt finding out such a small but intimate detail about him. 'How about you?'

'Hmm? Oh, are there many people here I know? Well, there's you and, uh, well, Jana, but I'd hardly call us lifelong friends.'

Matt smiled. 'You know what I mean. Friends? Siblings? Your parents?' He lowered his tone and looked at her over the top of his cup. 'I want to know more about Kelly O'Shea.'

She tilted her head to one side. 'I thought we agreed we weren't going to get involved.'

'Asking questions isn't getting involved.'

'Asking *personal* questions is!'

He replaced his cup and took another mouthful. 'Indulge me. Just this once.'

'All right, but fair is fair. Five questions each.'

He nodded his agreement.

'You can go first.'

'Do you have any siblings?'

'No.'

'When was the last time you saw your parents?'

'Two years ago but only for about ten minutes.' At his raised eyebrows she expanded. 'We bumped into each other at the airport terminal.'

He frowned. 'You don't see them regularly?'

'No.'

'Why not?'

Kelly shrugged. 'We just don't. It's not that we're not close—we are.'

'Oh, yeah, sure. I can see that,' he mocked.

She smiled. 'Not in a conventional way. The last time I lived with them, I was seventeen. I started med school at eighteen and moved to Sydney. My parents were in South America at the time.'

'Why do they move so often?'

'They're doctors who work in disaster areas,' she explained softly.

'Ah.' Matt nodded as though everything made sense. 'They go wherever there's a landslide or mudslide.'

'Or earthquake or collapsed buildings. Yes. That kind of thing.'

'With travelling so much as a child, I'm surprised you didn't want to settle down when you got older.'

'Me, too, but med school soon knocked that out of me. By the time I'd finished my internship, I was ready to bolt.'

'Was that when you met your ex-husband?'

Kelly took a soothing sip of her tea. There was that *tone* in his voice again. The one which said he didn't like the fact she'd been involved with someone else. It wasn't only jealousy she heard and saw but a bit of possessiveness as well. Usually, any sort of possessive behaviour made her run the other way, but with Matt the emotion suited him. She waggled her finger at him and smiled. 'Oh, no, you don't. You've had your five questions. Now it's my turn.'

Matt rubbed his fingers back and forth along his forehead, looking down at his empty plate before meeting her gaze once more. 'OK.'

'What do you wear to bed?'

'Pardon?'

'You heard.'

He cleared his throat. 'Nothing.'

'Now, that does surprise me.'

'Why?'

'Uh-uh-uh! It's *my* turn to ask the questions.' Kelly knew she had the advantage. She already knew about Matt's family and his upbringing so didn't need to waste any of her questions on things like that.

'What's your perfect honeymoon destination?'

Matt raised his cup to his lips and took a sip, hoping to stall for a few seconds. She was enjoying herself and he would by no means dispel her pleasure by not answering truthfully. He put his cup down and placed his elbows on the table, leaning his chin on his hands. It brought their faces closer together. 'Somewhere with good room service,' he finally replied, and wasn't at all surprised by the huskiness of his voice.

It was Kelly's turn to swallow, her eyes widening with pleasure. He loved it when that happened and he liked being the cause of it.

'Good. Uh, I mean…uh…good answer.'

'Next question?'

Kelly needed to get the upper hand once more to gain some vestige of control in this little game they were playing.

'If you could kiss me right now, where on my body would that kiss land?'

This was sheer torture, Matt thought, forcing his gaze to remain on hers. 'Your stomach.'

'Really? Why?'

'Because I'm intrigued by the miracle within you.'

Tears gathered in her eyes at his words. It was possibly the nicest thing anyone had ever said to her.

'Hey.' His tone changed from one of seductive teasing to one of concern. He reached out a hand as someone burst into the room, bringing the chill of the cold weather from outside.

'There's been an accident,' someone yelled in a loud and panicky voice.

CHAPTER SIX

KELLY and Matt sprang to their feet the instant the words were out of the man's mouth.

'Jana, call the State Emergency Service,' he instructed as he stalked over to the man. 'Come and sit down and tell us calmly what's happened.' The man was in a complete dither, shaking and upset.

'M-my friend, Abby, was… We were doing cross-country and, well, she's not that experienced at it and…well, we were trying to make it back before it got too dark, but…' He trailed off and started to cry. 'She's fallen. Down a cliff,' he said between hiccups.

Someone thrust a glass of brandy at the man and Matt advised him to take slow and calming sips. Someone else brought a few blankets to warm him up. Outside, Matt knew the staff were already getting things together for the start of the rescue.

'I…I wanted to go down to her. I could hear her crying but I couldn't see.' His tone was apologetic and Matt patted him reassuringly on the shoulder.

'You've done the right thing by coming here. Which track were you on?' The man didn't answer and Matt repeated the question. 'We need to know where you were so we can get to Abby.' Again the man was silent, tears streaming down his cheeks, his body shaking. Kelly noticed he was about to drop the glass of brandy and she quickly took it from him, holding it up to his mouth.

'What's your name?' she asked softly, after he'd taken a tiny sip.

'Carl.'

'I'm Kelly. This is my friend Matt and we're both doctors. Matt knows this area like the back of his hand so if you could tell us where you and Abby were, we can go and get her.'

'Will…will she be all right?' Carl turned worried eyes towards Kelly.

'We don't know, Carl. We won't know until we get to her, but the sooner we do that, the better.'

He shook his head sadly. 'I reached for her. I tried to get her but it was too late.'

'I understand,' Kelly soothed. 'But Abby's going to be in good hands. The SES are on their way. They have the heavy equipment we might need to use.'

Someone handed Matt a map of the area with the cross-country trails marked on it. 'Can you show us which one you were on, Carl?'

Carl nodded and wiped his cheeks before looking at the map. Moments later, his eyes blurred with tears again. 'I don't know. I don't know which one it is.'

'Which way did you come in?' Matt asked. 'Did you come here through the car-park?'

Carl thought. Kelly felt sorry for him. He was so distraught he had probably walked here on autopilot but until they had narrowed the search area, there was no point in anyone going outside just yet.

'Yes. Yes. I remember stumbling through the car-park. I flicked off my skis. They're outside. One of them broke. One broke when I was trying to lean over the cliff to get Abby.' He gazed off into the distance.

Matt started talking about other landmarks and Carl nodded. From what Carl was saying, it appeared they'd skied way off the cross-country track but at least Matt now had a fair idea of where Abby might be. Leaving Carl to the care of others, Matt took the map to another table.

He was in charge, Kelly thought as she watched him

speak to people, choosing volunteers for their abilities. Some of the staff members were a natural choice, but when he didn't give her an area Kelly frowned up at him.

'What's the deal? I'm coming, too!'

'No, you're not,' he said as he headed for the door.

'Matt? I'm a doctor and I'm a good skier. I may not know the terrain as well as some of the others but I'll be more help to you than sitting here.'

He rounded on her. 'You're pregnant,' he said in a stage whisper.

'So? I'm not an invalid. I'm more than capable.'

'I'm not going to let you risk it.'

'What's there to risk? I promise I'll do everything you say.'

'Kelly—'

'I've participated in rescues like this in several countries. Remember my parents? The first time I helped them in a ski rescue I was fourteen years old. I can abseil and rock-climb.'

'You're not going to—'

'I'm coming, Matt, and there's nothing you can do about it.' Kelly stormed off towards the others who were getting suited up with skis and other equipment.

Matt growled at her retreating back. 'Stubborn woman,' he said between clenched teeth.

Kelly turned and smiled at him. 'You'd better believe it, honey!'

The next hour passed quite quickly. Matt was in charge of the mission as he was a card-carrying member of the volunteer SES, which operated out of Bright. He split people up into teams to increase the chances of finding Abby sooner. He insisted Kelly be in his team. 'So I can keep an eye on you,' he murmured. Kelly wasn't going to complain.

As they set out, the teams kept in close communication not only with each other but with the SES via walkie-talkie, letting them know the present status and their current position. It was their team who eventually found Abby and they radioed through her whereabouts.

Matt called down to her but received no response.

'Get back from the edge,' Matt instructed. 'I don't want anyone going near that ledge unless they're wearing a safety harness and are attached to the safety lines.'

When the SES crew arrived, they started unloading their equipment. They sent a man down to find Abby's exact location. When he found her, he reported the position.

Kelly studied the equipment. 'A Larkin frame. Very impressive.'

'What did you expect?' Matt asked briskly as he helped unload the stuff. 'Our SES crew is well equipped.' Kelly went to help as well but the glare he gave her said otherwise. 'No, Kelly. No lifting.'

'All right.' She held up her gloved hands in self-defence. 'And I wasn't criticising anyone, I was merely making a statement. It's good to see crews well equipped and the Larkin frame is one of the best.'

'I take it you've used one before?'

'Of course.' She frowned at the question.

'Well, you're one up on the rest of us,' said the SES controller. 'I'm Jim,' he added, and Kelly shook his hand. 'We've only used it in training routines, never in an actual rescue.'

The wind started to blow, making its bitterly cold presence felt. 'I'm sure we're all going to be just fine,' she responded positively. Kelly helped them get the anchor support organised before they set up the Z-pulley at the rear. She adhered to Matt's instructions not to do any lifting but was able to hold things in place. Besides, moving around helped to keep them all warm.

Once everything was in place, a stretcher was attached to the pulley ropes, ready to be lowered down. Kelly walked over to where Matt was talking to Jim. 'What's the problem?' she asked, noting their concerned looks.

'We need someone with more than first-aid training to go down to Abby,' Matt answered.

'Well, why don't you go, Matt?'

'Because I haven't been trained on the Larkin frame yet.' He raked his hand through his hair and Kelly nodded, realising his dilemma.

'You want me to go,' she stated.

'Yes.' He turned to face her, placing his hands on her shoulders. 'I don't want to put the baby in danger but…' he shook his head '…if I don't, we risk Abby's life.'

'I'm more than happy to go down, Matt. I've used the equipment several times before, and I promise to take every precaution necessary to protect not only myself but the baby and my patient as well.'

Matt nodded, his expression grim. Kelly smiled up at him. 'Everything will be fine,' she prophesied.

'Decision reached,' Jim said triumphantly. 'Let's get you ready, Kelly.'

Kelly stood for a split second looking up at Matt, realising how hard it had been for him to put her in this situation. For some reason he felt responsible for her, and at the moment Kelly wasn't exactly sure how she felt about that. She'd always been responsible for herself. It was a strange sensation and one that almost overwhelmed her.

She reached up and brushed a soft kiss across Matt's lips. 'Thanks for caring,' she whispered, before heading over to the stretcher.

Matt found it hard to pull his gaze away from her as she tugged a pair of large orange overalls over her ski-suit before stepping into an abseiling harness and attaching the D-clamp and the winch ropes. Seeing her doing this so expertly should have helped the knot of dread in his gut to loosen, but it didn't.

She changed out of her ski-boots into a pair of heavy boots that had to be stuffed with socks so they would fit her, and a medical kit was strapped to her chest. She was really going to do this. He walked over and listened as she was given last-minute instructions, working hard to push away his personal feelings. They were professionals. She put the headset in place so they could communicate with her the entire time and accepted a pair of thick leather gloves from Matt.

'Thanks.' She smiled at him, her eyes alive with excitement as well as concentration. 'Check, check,' she said into the microphone that hovered near her mouth.

'Gotcha,' Jim replied, raising a hand to his ear. 'Let's get moving before this wind picks up even more.' He gave the signal to start the winch.

Kelly looked at Matt who simply stared at her as she headed out towards the edge, the basket stretcher also linked to the winch ropes. She turned so her back was to the drop and soon found herself dangling in mid-air, the winch holding both herself and the stretcher. She sat back in her harness, quite comfortable.

The SES had rigged up lights to shine down to the rescue site but still it was very dark. The winch moved carefully but steadily downwards. Kelly angled her head, the light from her helmet picking up the rockface before her.

'Not much further now,' she heard someone say into the headset. She glanced down and across and spotted the ledge where the SES worker stood in overalls identical to hers, the patient lying at his feet. 'The ledge is quite wide,' she remarked, knowing Jim and the people above could hear everything she and the other SES worker were saying.

The guy reached for the stretcher and soon her feet were safely on terra firma. 'At least we can fit the stretcher and Abby side by side,' she remarked. She unhooked herself from the stretcher but remained hooked up to the winch.

Kneeling by Abby's side, she called, 'Abby? Can you hear me?' Abby groaned, which was a good sign. 'Abby, my name is Kelly. I'm a doctor and we're here to help you.'

Again a groan. 'She's conscious.' Kelly took off her gloves, stuffing them down the front of her overalls, and pulled off the medical kit. It had everything she needed, including a small vial of morphine. She took out her medical torch and checked Abby's eyes. 'Pupils equal and reacting to light.' She checked her carotid pulse. 'Pulse is slow but firm.' She drew up a shot of morphine and administered it, all the time telling Abby what she was doing. 'This will help with the pain,' she said.

'There's no point in checking for fractures through this ski-suit,' she reported as she packed things away and pulled her gloves on again. 'We're ready to get her into the stretcher.' She fitted a neck brace around Abby's neck to help keep her head stable in case of spinal injuries.

'All right, Abby. It's time to move. Abby? Can you hear me?' Kelly said again.

The woman groaned. 'I'm sc-scared,' Abby stuttered, her teeth chattering.

'I know, but we're almost there. Once you're in the stretcher, the worst part will be over. Promise.'

'C-Carl?'

'Carl's fine.' Kelly was glad to hear Abby asking after him. It showed she was coherent. With careful manoeuvering, Kelly and the SES worker managed to get Abby into the stretcher.

'There. The hard bit's over.' Kelly grasped the other woman's gloved hand and squeezed. 'You did well,' she praised as she tucked a warm space blanket around the woman.

Tears started to gather in Abby's eyes and Kelly knew she had to work fast. The SES worker secured the straps on the stretcher and Kelly made sure her medical kit was strapped firmly to her chest. 'Abby's in the stretcher, Jim, I'm hooked on and we're ready to rock 'n' roll.' Another line was attached to the foot of the stretcher, which would be controlled from below on the ledge. This helped stop the stretcher from spinning as it ascended, making it more comfortable for the patient.

'Start the winch,' she heard Jim say, and soon the slack on the ropes became taut.

'Here we go,' she said. The other woman whimpered. 'Just lie still and relax. This is the easy part where we don't have to do any work.' Another whimper. 'How's the pain?'

'I'm n-numb.'

'Not surprising, but at least you're not experiencing any pain. That's good.' Kelly reached out and laid a hand on Abby's forehead. 'Close your eyes. It'll all be over soon,' she said compassionately.

Kelly could see the top of the cliff and shielded her eyes against the bright lights which were shining around them. They were brought up and over the edge and soon the stretcher was being lowered to the ground.

Matt was one of the first people she saw and she smiled brightly at him. 'Long time, no see.' She laughed. His gaze was only on her for a second but the look he gave her warmed her through and through.

'Get that stretcher into the rear of one of the SES vehicles,' Matt ordered. 'Kelly, as soon as you're out of that gear, come and give me a hand.' He turned his attention to Abby. 'Hi Abby. I'm Matt, Kelly's colleague. We're going to get you sorted out.'

Abby murmured a noncoherent reply. 'Morphine's working,' Kelly stated as she unhooked herself and started climbing out of the harness. She removed the shoes, orange overalls and the gloves before heading over to where Matt was cutting off Abby's snow-suit as well as the rest of her clothes.

'Do her obs, Kelly. I'll check her bones.'

'Right.' Kelly reached into the SES emergency medical kit and pulled out a pair of gloves. She handed a pair to Matt before finding the medical torch.

They worked in harmony. 'Pupils are still equal and re-acting to light. Pulse is the same.' She pulled out the portable sphygmomanometer and wrapped the cuff around her patient's arm. 'BP ninety over forty.'

'Get an IV line in,' he mumbled before turning to call out, 'Can someone get this vehicle started and the heater on, please, so the patient can start to breathe in warm air?' No sooner were the words out of his mouth than his request was fulfilled.

'Arms all right?' Kelly waited for his nod and checked the pulse in both of Abby's arms to ensure there were no neurovascular blockages. 'Good.' She started getting the IV in, knowing they needed to boost Abby's fluids.

'Left ankle has puffed up like a balloon since I took her boot off. Right one appears to be fine. Left femur feels fractured, which is probably the cause of her low BP.'

'Oh, those bleeding femurs,' Kelly responded drolly.

'They feel fine at the moment but as her skin's so cold I don't want to press too much. I'll order the X-rays when we get to the hospital.'

'Cranial?'

'Yes. Chances are she's hit her head on the way down.'

'But at least she's regained consciousness and she was asking after Carl, so that's a good sign.'

'True.' They worked quickly together, trying desperately to warm Abby's cold flesh. Soon their driver appeared and they started off slowly down the mountain. 'Obs every five minutes,' Matt instructed, and Kelly nodded. She checked the neck brace they'd put around Abby's neck to ensure her head was stable during the ride. Her BP started to rise with the increased fluids and Kelly did neurological and neuro-vascular obs, reporting her findings.

When they arrived at Bright hospital, the staff were ready and waiting. 'Call an orthopod in,' Matt said, but Kelly stopped him.

'It's all right. I have a diploma in orthopaedics. I can fix her fractures.'

Matt stared at her for a full second before nodding. 'Let's get her X-rayed. Kelly, go and grab a quick cup of tea and sit down for a few minutes before you get changed.'

'I'm fine.' She waved away his concern but the glare he gave her made her change her mind. 'Good idea. Think I'll sit down for a few minutes.'

'Thank you.' Matt headed off with their patient to Radiology. He'd forgotten about Kelly's extra qualifications. Kelly O'Shea was no simple GP. In fact, he doubted if she ever did *anything* simply.

Kelly was glad of his advice, especially after she took her first sip of the hot cup of tea, feeling it spread throughout her. 'Ah.' She sat down and stretched a little, surprised to find a yawn working its way up and out. Resting a hand on her flat tummy, she whispered, 'How are you doing, darling?'

As she moved her arm to pick up her cup, she realised the bulkiness of her ski-suit would probably get in the way during Theatre and smiled to herself as she stood. She was just pulling down the zipper when Matt walked into the room.

He couldn't move. The sight of Kelly unzipping her suit, peeling it back as he'd longed to do ever since he'd first laid eyes on her that day, made the previous coldness leave his body and a heat, fuelled by desire, burn through him. He'd already removed his own suit and changed into theatre scrubs but stood stock still, completely mesmerised by her actions.

Their gazes held as Kelly continued. She slowed the pace down, knowing he was enjoying the performance. She lifted one shoulder and slid her arm from the sleeve. Then she repeated the action on the other side. The excitement of what she was doing started to burn deep within her and her breathing accelerated.

Matt swallowed.

She slid it down to her waist to reveal a black turtleneck jumper beneath. She lifted her hands up to her hair and took the beanie off, letting her mass of red curls fall over her shoulders. Next, she bent to remove her ski-boots.

He was loving every second of it.

He watched as she removed one boot and then the other, her height being lowered by a few inches. But it didn't matter to him, not in the slightest. From the kisses they'd shared, he knew she fitted perfectly into his arms at the height she was, without any shoes.

The rest of her suit was about to be expelled and she wriggled from side to side in order to achieve this.

Matt gaped.

She pulled the suit first over one leg, then the other, revealing black woollen leggings and thick socks. When she straightened, she shook her head, the contrast of her red curls on the black clothes that hugged her body even more sensual than the red and black ski suit had been.

Slowly she reached for the cup, realising she was trembling slightly. Her heart was pounding wildly in her ears, yet she could still hear the hard rasps of Matt's breaths filling the room. Raising the teacup to her lips, she didn't break eye contact and took a sip of the warm tea. Replacing the cup on the table, she slowly walked over to Matt and stood before him. Then she reached up and pushed his lower jaw closed.

She wanted nothing more than to have his mouth on hers

to repeat those amazing kisses they'd already shared, but she knew she couldn't. Not yet!

'Back to business,' she said, unable to control her husky tone. She cleared her throat. 'Concentrate, Matt.' She turned, finally breaking the mesmerising look they'd shared the whole time she'd been removing her suit. It was the sexiest thing she'd ever done for a man and she'd loved every minute of it.

'You've got to be kidding.' His words were a hoarse whisper and when she turned to look over her shoulder at him, he still appeared to be glued to the spot. 'How's a man supposed to think logically after a performance like that?'

Kelly laughed, glad she'd been able to knock the logic out of him—even if it had only been for a second. She drained her cup and took it to the sink. He still hadn't moved. She returned to his side.

'Come on. We have a patient to care for and if I'm going to find the offending blood vessels that are doing the damage, I need all distractions removed—and that includes sensual thoughts of *you*.' She took a deep breath and slowly released it. 'I presume you hold a diploma in general surgery?'

Matt exhaled slowly and nodded. 'Yes.' He covered his eyes with one hand for a moment, as though he was desperately trying to get control of his thoughts. A moment later he removed it and looked down at Kelly.

'So you're all right to assist me?'

He nodded again, this time with more control. 'Absolutely. I'll go and see how they're getting on in Radiology.'

'Good. I'll go get into theatre scrubs.' They both walked out of the room, heading in separate directions. That's the way it has to be, Kelly thought—separate directions, separate lives. She would love to explore this attraction she felt for Matt simply because he made her feel like no other man had, and although it scared her, it was an exciting yet scary feeling. One that grew with each second they spent together.

Half an hour later, they stood opposite each other with the patient between them on the operating table. Kelly was concentrating on the operation, not at all surprised to find how well she and Matt worked together in Theatre. 'There it is,' she said triumphantly. 'Nasty little bleeder. Suction.'

'Suction,' he repeated.

'Clamp.'

'Clamp.' He placed the instrument firmly into her out-stretched palm.

'The break's quite clean, really. We'll be inserting some plates and screws...' she put a temporary suture into the artery as she spoke '...which should stabilise Abby's fracture without a problem.'

'How many fractured femurs have you fixed?' one of the nurses asked.

Matt had to admit he was curious about Kelly's expertise because she certainly could have become an orthopaedic surgeon with the skills she was displaying.

'About a hundred,' she replied.

'And you're not an orthopod.'

'No.' She laughed. 'There's no way I could do this for a living. Not enough variety. Bones are just bones and although there are different techniques and methods to fix different types of fractures, there's no...*verve* in it.'

'*Verve?*' Matt raised his eyebrows and looked at her. He could tell by the way her green eyes twinkled that she was smiling beneath her mask.

'Yes. Verve. Something wrong with that?'

'No. No. Nothing wrong.' It explained a lot about her, Matt thought as they continued with the operation. Kelly was a person who obviously didn't like the same old routine, in the same old place with the same old people. Was this why she moved so often?

But what about her ex-husband? She'd been married to him for five years. Surely that showed she could commit to something? Or someone?

He was amazed with her skills and techniques as she plated Abby's femur back together. She was way too qualified to be just a general practitioner. She could do further training, teach students, share her experiences, but instead she'd chosen to come to Bright. Sleepy little Bright, and right now he was glad she had.

When the operation was over, he found her sitting in the kitchenette with her feet up on a chair, drinking a glass of water. She was still wearing theatre scrubs and the baggy green cotton enhanced her already gorgeous eyes.

'Feeling OK?'

'Yeah, just tired.' She yawned as though to prove it. 'I was just trying to summon the energy to get up, change and get out of here. Then I remembered my car is still up in the Mount Buffalo car park.'

Matt nodded and picked up her feet, sitting down in the chair where they'd been resting. He started to massage them through the thick black socks. He expected her to relax, to give a deep sigh and appreciate how wonderful it was. Instead, he realised she was tensing even more. When he turned to look at her, he found both hands clamped over her mouth and her shoulders gently shaking.

'What's wrong?' He was instantly alert. Was she hurt?

Kelly removed her hands from her mouth, glad he'd stopped moving his hands over her ticklish feet. She giggled and shook her head. 'No. No.' She gasped for breath. 'Nothing's wrong.'

'You're ticklish,' he realised, a slow smile spreading across his face. 'Why didn't you say so?'

'I didn't want to spoil your good deed. Far be it from me to stop you from getting your foot massage badge at Scouts.'

'So you would have suffered in silence?' He moved his fingers slightly and she jumped.

'Y-yes.' She laughed. 'Oh, yes.'

'I see.' He stopped moving his fingers and Kelly lifted her legs off his lap.

'What do you see?'

He looked at her closely. 'I see a woman who's extremely tired and needs some sleep.' He stood. 'Come on, let's check on Abby and then I'll take you home.'

'But *your* car's up on Mount Buffalo as well,' she pointed out.

'I know.' He held out a hand and gently helped her to her feet. 'Let's see how our patient is.'

'Good idea.' He held her hand for a fraction of a second longer than was necessary, not that Kelly minded.

Abby was stable and would be transferred to Wangaratta hospital tomorrow morning after one of them had reviewed her.

'I'll do it,' Matt volunteered.

'It's all right, Matt. I'm more than happy to do it if some-one can give me a lift to the hospital.'

'The SES boys will bring your car back down as soon as possible,' one of the nurses told her. 'They're good like that, aren't they, Matt?'

'Absolutely. Don't stress about it, Kelly. I'm more than happy to come in and get the paperwork organised, as well as making sure Abby's condition is stable. Thanks to you, her blood pressure is almost back to normal, her ankle is strapped and the hypothermia is under control. No skull fractures, no upper limb fractures. She's been one lucky lady.'

'And her boyfriend has just arrived,' one of the nurses said.

'There you go. She's got it all, so why don't you sleep in tomorrow and let me take the call?'

'I did the surgery.'

'She's been signed in under both of us and I think I know what I'm looking for.'

'I'm not saying you don't, but the fact remains that I did the surgery so I'll be here tomorrow morning to check on her.'

'Then it looks as though we're both coming.'

'I guess so.'

'I suppose you'll want a lift, then.'

'Yes.'

'Go and get changed and meet me at the front reception desk in five minutes. I'll go check on Carl.' He nodded dismissively before walking from the room.

Kelly shook her head, blaming his over-protective urge as well as fatigue on the way they were both behaving. 'I guess we'll see you in the morning,' she told the nursing staff, before heading to the changing rooms.

She dressed in her black outfit once more and pulled the ski-suit back on as she didn't have a coat and had heard one of the nurses say that it had started to rain. Matt was waiting for her, also dressed in his own ski-suit. 'I've admitted Carl overnight for observation.'

'Good. A situation is usually worse for the person who's *not* going through it but watching from the sidelines.'

Matt looked at her for a moment, wondering whether there was a double meaning hidden there somewhere, but when she didn't say anything else he made a sweeping bow and said, 'Your chariot awaits, *Madame.*'

'*Merci,*' she replied, and placed her hand into the one he offered. His left arm came around her body and he held her close. Nice move, she thought. She leaned closer into him and he accepted the shift.

'I don't want you to slip out here,' he murmured in her ear.

Kelly stopped in her tracks, making him stop, too, and glared up at him. 'What?'

'I said I didn't want you to accidentally slip. This way, we're supporting each other.' His grip tightened a little and he urged her on. She let him.

'So whose car are we stealing?'

'No one's. I checked with the SES guys and they said to take their four-wheel-drive. With the roads being this wet, I'll admit it makes a lot of sense.'

'Nice and safe,' she said drolly, as he unlocked the passenger door and held it open for her. She couldn't stand this any longer.

'Listen, Matt,' she said after he'd settled himself behind the wheel. 'I really appreciate your concern but…don't you think you're overdoing it a little?'

'No.' He started the engine, letting it idle to warm up. 'Someone's got to look out for you and you're not doing a very good job.'

'In your opinion,' she stated.

'Yes. In my opinion. A baby takes a lot of energy from the mother, especially in the first and third trimesters. Today you've done a clinic, been skiing, helped in a rescue and operated. Even without being pregnant, that's a lot.'

'So we're doctors. We're used to it.'

'Yes, but you're a pregnant doctor and you don't seem to be able to get that rammed into that red head of yours. I only volunteered to come in tomorrow so you could get more rest. You're going to need it,' he prophesied as he switched the car heater on. Soon warmth flooded them and Kelly leaned her head back against the headrest.

'Let *me* be the judge of what I need. How much sleep I need. What activities I undertake.'

'I also have a responsibility to the practice. You're in our employ and we'll be demanding a lot of you.'

'I know, and I'm more than happy to pull my weight.' A

thought struck her and she turned slightly in her chair to look at him. 'Don't you think I'm pulling my weight?'

'I think you're doing a great job—for now. But what happens in the next few months? You have morning sickness and it's already made you exhausted.'

'I know,' she groaned. 'But that isn't going to go on for ever and I wasn't late for clinic this morning.'

'It doesn't bother me too much, Kelly. I'm more concerned about your health than the clinics. I know plenty of women who have worked successfully through pregnancies in very demanding jobs—Rhea being one of them—but you need to make sure you take the necessary steps to ensure your baby's health.'

'Nothing could be more important to me, Matt. I've told you about the endometriosis. You know this baby is an absolute miracle and there's no way I'd let anything or anyone hurt it.'

Kelly said the words with a lot more vehemence than he thought was necessary, and it sparked a warning that there was something else going on which he didn't know about. He rounded the corner and pulled the vehicle into her driveway.

'Whose car is that?' he asked, the headlights picking up the flashy red of a Ferrari.

'Oh, no,' she groaned. 'This is just like him.'

'Like who?' Matt asked cautiously, instinctively knowing he wouldn't like the answer.

'Freddy.'

CHAPTER SEVEN

'I LEFT a message for him to call me back and what does he do? He drives up here instead. The man's a nutter.' Kelly shook her head, bemused. 'Thanks, Matt. I'll see you in the morning. Eight o'clock?'

'Eight.' His jaw was clenched, his expression blank. He gave a brisk nod and revved the engine loudly, hoping her ex was asleep. He reversed out of her driveway before driving along in front of his house and parking the SES vehicle in his garage.

Her ex was here.

'Excellent!' He punched the steering-wheel, feeling his frustrations rise up and swamp him. He wasn't prepared for this. No doubt the man would be staying a few days—and in the same house as Kelly. They'd been married for a long time so anything was possible.

Matt ground his teeth together, telling himself it was none of his business. Kelly had a lot of things to deal with and he wasn't one of them. So what if she kissed like a dream, if she felt perfect in his arms? It meant nothing. Her ex was here and there was nothing he could do about it.

Squaring his shoulders firmly, he opened the door and climbed from the vehicle, locking it securely behind him. The way he was feeling brought back memories of when Louise had come and gone from his life within a short space of time. Slowly making his way inside, not caring that the rain was now pelting down, Matt went to the kitchen and switched on the kettle.

Usually when he started to reflect on his relationship with Louise, the vivacious strawberry blonde who had set him firmly in her sights, all he felt was annoyance at his own stupidity. Although tonight was no exception, the feelings weren't as strong as they usually were.

He raked a hand through his wet hair and shook his head. Louise had come for the ski season the year after he'd broken up with Jana. She'd been working at the chalet, which was where they'd met, and they'd instantly hit it off. She'd urged him to throw caution to the winds, to let go, and as he was a man on the rebound, he'd listened. It had also helped that Jana had seemed incredibly jealous of Louise. Now, four years on, he knew his actions had been nothing but vanity mixed with a healthy dose of stupidity.

Louise had left at the end of two months, even though Matt had tried to persuade her to stay. Afterwards, he'd vowed never to enter into a relationship again until he was sure the woman in question was prepared to stick around permanently—as his wife.

He wanted to get married, to have a family and to raise his family here in Bright. The kettle boiled and he made himself a soothing cup of tea, carrying it through to his study. He walked over to his desk, switching on the small lamp which illuminated the papers neatly stacked around the edge.

His answering-machine light blinked and he pressed the button.

'Hi Matt, it's Natasha. Everything's set for Monday for the hearing test. I'll catch up with you later. Bye.'

Matt sat down in his chair and leaned back thoughtfully. Natasha Forest. Now, there was a woman he classified as perfect marriage and family material. She'd been married twice before, he'd known one of her husbands very well and, of course, there was her daughter Lily. They'd been friends for years and he cared for both Natasha and Lily quite deeply.

'But you don't love her,' he said out loud. He listened to

the rain for a few minutes, knowing he could never marry someone he didn't love with all his heart. He'd had the example of his parents' marriage. He refused to settle for anything less.

He closed his eyes and breathed deeply, a vision of Kelly popping into his head. She was different from Jana and Louise. She wasn't trying to change him into something he wasn't, she merely accepted him for who he was.

She could make him hot simply by wiggling those sexy hips of hers. That strip-tease today had almost tipped him over the edge. He'd wanted nothing more at that moment than to sweep her up into his arms and beg for more.

Instead, they'd both cooled down and had operated on Abby like the professionals they were. Professionals. Medical colleagues. He admired her skill, her intelligence and her vivacity. Sharing his work with her was something he hadn't found with either Jana or Louise, and it was definitely a bonus.

But, like Louise, she would be leaving. Moving on to a new place, new people and a new life with her child. He wondered how she would tell her ex-husband about the baby, and what the other man's reaction would be.

'This won't get the work done,' he growled, and sat forward in his chair. He sipped at his tea and looked at his paperwork. When he'd read the same paragraph four times over, he decided to give up. Reaching forward, he switched off the light and turned to close his curtains.

His hand was gripping the material, ready to pull it closed, when the light in Kelly's room came on. She walked in with a man following her. He was tall and blond and Matt instantly disliked him. He watched as Kelly pointed back to the doorway, giving him a gentle shove.

When he protested, she turned and grabbed a blanket and pillow off her bed and gave them to him. He hung his head but left nonetheless. Once he'd gone, she closed the door and leaned against it.

Matt let out the breath he'd been unconsciously holding.

She looked out the window and for an instant Matt thought she'd spotted him. His heart started to pound fiercely against his ribs and a flash of heat spread over his body. His mouth went dry as she slowly walked over to the window and peered out.

She looked directly into his house. Into his study. Through his own open curtains. He wasn't sure whether she could see him or not but knew that if he moved, the light from the hallway behind him would pick up on his shadow.

Matt slowly let out his breath, staying as still as a statue, waiting…waiting to see what she did next.

Kelly raised her fingers to her lips and then blew him a kiss before reaching out and closing the curtains.

Had she seen him?

Now that Matt could move, he found he was unable to. He stayed there, looking out his window at the rim of light that peeked from the side of the curtains just in case she opened them quickly and saw him moving—catching him in the act.

Had she seen him?

Did it matter?

Surprisingly, Kelly slept very well that night, even though she was conscious of having Freddy under the same roof.

She hadn't been able to believe he'd suggested they sleep in the same bed. She shook her head as she nibbled at a piece of dry toast and sipped her peppermint tea. It just pointed out quite clearly how different they'd become. Perhaps they'd always been different but Kelly hadn't wanted to notice because she'd been too busy burying herself in her work, trying to compete on the good deed level with her parents.

Freddy had been willing to come along for the ride and he'd been a charming and handsome distraction. When he'd suggested they get married at the end of their internship, she'd readily agreed, thinking it would be a hoot as well as annoying his parents. She'd found out later that Freddy had also received a sizeable sum of money on their marriage, and although it had mildly annoyed her that he hadn't told her about it before their wedding, it hadn't bothered her too much. She didn't need Freddy's money and had always kept their accounts separate, in the fail-safe that if his parents ever accused her of being a gold-digger or marrying Freddy for his money, then she could prove them wrong.

She'd been young. She'd wanted to travel and she'd wanted someone to do it with so she could be just like her parents. She could help people out and still have a personal relationship with a man. Freddy had been a good friend and they'd had a great time together, but then she'd started to change. Kelly now realised she'd grown up and Freddy had stayed…well…Freddy.

Kelly sighed and took another bite of her toast, checking the time. It was almost eight o'clock and she didn't want to keep Matt waiting. She thought of leaving a note for Freddy but decided against it. He'd probably still be asleep when she got back and then they could have their chat. The last thing she wanted was for Freddy to hang around.

Trying to eat faster only resulted in her feeling queasy so she donned her coat and scarf and picked up her bag and the mug before hurrying out the door. She met Matt on the path between their houses.

'I was just coming over to get you.' His tone was mildly impatient.

'Here I am,' she replied chirpily. 'How are you this morning?' She sipped her tea.

'Fine. Running late?' He gestured to the cup. He'd been in a foul mood since he'd got up, wondering how long her ex-husband planned on staying in Bright, yet a few seconds in her company and he found himself relaxing. Still, he remembered to hold himself in check. She had a lot to deal with at the moment and didn't need him complicating things even more.

'No, just can't eat or drink too quickly.'

'Sleep well?' he enquired as they headed around to the SES vehicle. Matt unlocked the passenger door and held it open for her.

'Actually, I did, and I haven't had any morning sickness this morning.'

His gaze met hers and he smiled. 'Glad to hear it. Tea smells nice.'

'Mmm.' She took another sip.

Matt went around to the driver's side and climbed in. 'Let's go see how the patients are.'

Kelly nodded, cradling the mug between her hands. 'How about you? Did you sleep well?'

'Ah, yes. Better than normal.'

'You haven't been sleeping well lately?' Kelly thought that sounded very promising and hoped she was the cause of it. She'd stared into his study window last night, wishing she could be over there with him, the two of them snuggled together in front of the fire as they wound down from the night's excitement.

The thought had continued on into her dreams where she and Matt lived together in his house. Worked together, side by side. Raised their kids together, laughing and disciplining the brood, especially the little girl with the red curls and mischievous eyes like her mother.

It was the perfect picture of domestication and Kelly had woken feeling relaxed and refreshed. It was then she'd realised that the picture painted hadn't scared her. She hadn't been bothered by it. Instead, she'd embraced the change from the hectic pace she'd been living all her life.

When they pulled up at the hospital, Kelly was still sipping tea as she carried it inside. 'Good morning,' she greeted the nursing staff cheerfully. 'How are the patients?'

'Abby's doing fine. Once she knew Carl was all right and nearby, she settled down quite nicely,' the sister reported.

'Glad to hear it.' Matt nodded.

'How about Carl?' Kelly asked. 'Did *he* have a good night?'

Sister laughed. 'Once he realised Abby was really all right, he settled down as well, although he did wake around three o'clock with a nightmare.'

'It's to be expected. He might need some counselling,' Kelly stated.

'I'll make sure he has a referral.' Matt made a note of it in Carl's file.

They checked both their patients and Kelly was pleased with the way Abby had responded to the surgery. 'We'll be transferring you to Wangaratta hospital this morning,' Kelly said.

'Why can't I stay here?' Abby asked, her face bruised and scratched in several places.

'Because you need to see an orthopaedic surgeon.'

'Aren't you one? You did my operation.'

'That's correct, but I only hold a diploma in orthopaedics. You'll be fine,' she reassured. 'Carl will be going with you and as soon as the orthopaedic surgeon is satisfied with your condition, you'll be able to head back home to Melbourne.'

'Some holiday,' Abby grumbled.

'You'll get through it. I hope this experience won't put you off skiing altogether.'

'Perhaps the next time you're in the snow,' Matt said, 'you might want to try something a bit more gentle, like tobogganing on a small slope or gentle skiing, rather than cross-country.'

'Hrumph. Maybe,' Abby sulked. Kelly really couldn't

blame her. This would be remembered as a lousy holiday but if people turned their perspectives around, she hoped it would be a time of change in their lives—focusing on the fact that they'd survived a terrible accident and had lived to experience more of life.

Matt completed the paperwork and once the ambulance had come to take their patients off to Wangaratta, Kelly and Matt headed back home.

'That wasn't so bad.' Matt smiled.

'Abby's still not too pleased about all this happening to her.'

'Time's a great healer of all wounds, physical, emotional and mental.'

'That's good advice,' she said softly.

'Have you told him yet?'

'No.' She took a deep breath and slowly let it out. 'I'm mentally psyching myself up for it now.'

'How's he going to react?'

'He'll blow his top. He'll probably ask if it's his.'

'Will he? Why else would you be telling him if it wasn't his?'

'Yeah, well, that's a bit too logical for Freddy.' Kelly laughed. 'Just park in your driveway, Matt. I can walk the rest of the way.'

He did as she'd suggested. When he'd cut the engine, he turned to face her. 'Are you going to be OK?'

'Sure. I've handled Freddy's tantrums for years.'

'I think I'd better come with you.'

'No, Matt. Bad idea.' She took a breath. 'I appreciate the sentiment, really I do, and you're a sweetheart for offering, but a girl's gotta do, what a girl's gotta do.'

'Well…all right, but you call me or come and get me if you need me. Promise.'

'I promise.'

'I'll walk you to the door.'

There it was, that protective urge again. 'Sure.' Neither of them spoke as they navigated the path, and when she opened the back door she heard female laughter coming from the direction of the kitchen. Both she and Matt rushed in.

Kelly put her mug down on the bench and stared at Rhea, who was sitting at the old kitchen table, wiping tears from her eyes. Freddy, dressed in a pair of denim jeans and a loose-fitting T-shirt, stood by the sink. He looked good— too good. Too…polished.

'Hey, there she is.' Freddy placed his arm about Kelly's shoulders. 'I was just telling Rhea about the time you—' He stopped when he saw Matt. 'Hi.' He offered Matt his free hand. 'Freddy Holdsworthy. You must be Matt.' For Kelly's sake and out of politeness, Matt shook the other man's hand, only just controlling the primal urge to break all his fingers.

Kelly shrugged out from beneath Freddy's arm and sat down in a chair. 'What brings you by, Rhea?'

'I came over to see how you were this morning and found a strange man wandering about in the kitchen. Where have you two been so early?'

'Hospital,' Matt replied, standing by the door. At Rhea's raised eyebrows, he said, 'Retrieval last night. One patient required surgery, the other admitted for observation. Current status—both patients are fine and on their way to Wangaratta.'

'Nice one.' Rhea nodded encouragingly. She looked from Matt to Kelly and then to Freddy, who was concentrating on making toast. 'Have you told him?' Rhea mouthed, and Kelly shook her head.

Freddy brought his toast to the table and sat down. After taking a bite, he looked at Kelly and swallowed. 'Sorry, Kel. Did you want some toast?'

'It's fine. I've already eaten.'

'Really?' Rhea raised her eyebrows. 'That's good to hear. Well, Matt, why don't you come and sit in my kitchen for a while and I'll make you some breakfast? Besides, the kids are dying to see you.'

'Sure,' Matt agreed reluctantly, and shot a pointed look at Kelly that said, You know where I am if you need me.

Kelly smiled and was about to stand when Matt walked by and placed a hand on her shoulder. 'Don't get up.' He gave it a little squeeze before leaving with Rhea.

'Nice family,' Freddy said once they'd gone, his mouth half-full of toast. 'Nothing like yours or mine, eh?'

'Yes. They're *very* nice. Listen, Freddy, I need to talk to you.' No time like the present, Kelly thought. The sooner she got it over and done with, the sooner he'd leave. She took a deep breath and closed her eyes for a moment, silently thinking of the best way to break it to him. She'd been thinking about this ever since she'd found out about the baby, but the right words hadn't yet formed.

'What is it, Kel? You can tell me.' He reached out and placed a hand over hers.

She opened her eyes and looked at him. 'I'm pregnant, Freddy.' The words came out in a calm and controlled manner and she gave herself brownie points for not rushing it.

He stared at her, open-mouthed. 'Wh-what?'

'I'm pregnant.'

'Wh-wh—? How? I mean, I know *how* but…but…*how*? I thought the endometriosis stopped you from—'

'Well, sometimes miracles happen, and this is one of those times.'

He was silent for a moment as though thinking things through. 'So that's what Rhea meant when she said she stopped by to check on you.' He nodded. 'Wow, Kelly. That's so great. I'm really happy for you. A baby. After all this time. What are you going to do? Where are you going to live?' He raised his hand to his chest. 'I'm really touched

you wanted to share this with me, Kel. It just shows that
we really can stay friends after a divorce.'

Kelly smiled politely and nodded. 'Freddy?' She cleared
her throat. 'You're the father.'

'What?' He jumped up so quickly from his chair that it
fell backwards. *'What?'* he roared again.

Kelly kept her smile in place. Here we go again. 'Sit
down, Freddy.'

'No.' He started to pace around the room. 'I'm the fath—
No. No.' He swatted the air with his hands as though trying
to push her words away. 'You've got to be wrong. It has to
be someone else, Kel. It has to be.'

'Why? Do you think I'm lying?' She kept her voice calm,
knowing if she raised her own it would take Freddy even
longer to calm down.

'We were together for so many years and you *never* got
pregnant. We knew we couldn't have kids and now…' He
thumped the wall.

'Hey, be careful. This isn't my house.'

'How can you be pregnant? It was that night, wasn't it?
The one before we signed the divorce papers? Is that what
you're telling me?'

'Yes.'

'Kelly, we'd been separated for a year. Are you sure you
weren't seeing someone else?'

'Freddy!' Kelly was having a hard time holding onto her
composure. He was all but accusing her of sleeping around.
'I'm not promiscuous, Freddy, and you of all people should
know that.'

'I know you wouldn't sleep with me until after we were
married.'

'Exactly.'

'But you sure know how to flirt. Maybe some guy got
you drunk and you don't remember and—'

'Stop!'

'What about…' he pointed to the back door that Matt and Rhea had just left by. '…that guy? The one you're working for now.'

'Matt?'

'Yeah, Matt. I noticed the chemistry between the two of you. They way he put his hand on your shoulder just now. Very possessive.'

'You think Matt got me drunk and had his…er…way with me, which has resulted in a pregnancy?'

'It might have happened.'

'Freddy, I've only been here for a week and I'm nine weeks pregnant. You may not believe this, but you are the only man I've slept with. Period. You and I are going to have a baby. End of story.'

Freddy sighed and bent over, his hands resting on his knees, his back arched and his head hanging low. He was silent for a moment before standing up straight again. 'You're really pregnant?'

'Why would I say it if I wasn't?'

'Because you want me back.'

'Be careful, Freddy. Your arrogance is showing.'

'Come on, Kel, what am I supposed to think?' he thundered. 'You know one of the reasons we got a divorce was that my family expect me to provide them with a male heir. I'm the only son, the only one who can carrying on the Holdsworthy name. You and I together were incompatible as far as baby production goes. You agreed to that as a reason for the divorce.'

'So now you think I want you back and pregnancy is the only way to do it? Why? Because of the family money?' Kelly's tone was deadly quiet and she saw Freddy's eyes widen in fear.

'No. I know you don't care about the money. You've never touched even a cent of it.' He'd lowered his tone to a more reasonable level.

'Then why, after a year of separation, would I pull a stunt like this just to get you back?'

'Because you were jealous?'

'Of what?' she asked incredulously.

Freddy frowned. 'You mean, you don't know?'

'Know what?'

'Me and Carmen Ristoro.'

'Who?'

'Honestly, Kel. Don't you read the papers?'

'I read about world events, not the gossip pages.'

'My parents and her parents want us to marry.'

'Congratulations,' Kelly said honestly.

'And now you say you're carrying my baby.' Freddy slumped down at the table and buried his head in his hands. 'What am I supposed to do? My parents are going to flip!'

'Well, the ball is in your court, Freddy. Tell them, don't tell them. I don't care, but know this. I'm not going to abort this baby and I'm not going to let anyone take it away from me.'

'But if it's a boy—'

'No one, Freddy. Boy or girl, this child is mine. You can have as much to do with it or as little to do with it as you like. I know once you tell your parents what they'd probably say about me, but know that this child was conceived within the bonds of matrimony. We were still legally married, which would mean that one day, if our child chooses, he or she will have the right to the Holdsworthy name and everything that goes with it. *If* our child chooses. If you *don't* want anything to do with the baby, I completely understand, but I won't lie to our child and hide the truth.'

'What if you remarry?'

'That has nothing to do with our child's birthright, Freddy, but if your parents even *try* to instigate court proceedings to claim custody of the child, I will fight them to the bitter end. They've messed with your life—and your sisters'—too much for my liking. I'm not going to let them ruin my child's. Is that perfectly clear?'

'Yes—and rightly so.' Freddy nodded. 'They're just so…scary sometimes.' He raised his head and looked at Kelly. She felt sorry for him, that much hadn't changed. He was like a little boy, caught in the power of his controlling parents.

'Do you like this Carmen Ristoro?'

'Yeah.' He shrugged. 'She's nice.'

'Freddy. Promise me one thing. Don't marry her unless you love her.'

'I loved you, Kel, and look how that ended.'

She smiled. 'Freddy, you loved me like a big sister. Someone who would fight your battles for you and help you escape from your problems. We never shared that deep, abiding love people write about. I may not see my parents that much but they have it—they love each other. Surely you saw that the few times you met them? They fought, they cried, they shared. They are each other's halves and together they make up one person. You and I were never like that, Freddy. Even though we kidded ourselves for a while, we were never like that.'

He nodded. 'I still love you, Kel, but you're right. Not that way.' He stood and shoved his hands into his pockets. 'But I need time to think. I promise not to say anything to my parents until I've spoken to you again.'

'All right.'

'I'll get packed and go.' He walked to the doorway of the kitchen and then turned back. 'Uh, Kel. Sorry about last night. I was only joking when I offered to sleep with you… Well…uh…if you'd said yes, I wouldn't have let you down, but I…uh…would have been surprised if you *had* agreed.'

Kelly picked up the closest thing to her, which was a teatowel, and threw it at him. He laughed as he caught it and threw it back. It landed on the table just in front of her. She watched him walk away and breathed a sigh of relief.

Freddy knew about the baby. Problem number one on her list taken care of. Now all she had to do was to figure out who was going to deliver the baby, where she was going to work once this contract expired and how she was going to work and raise a child on her own.

'Easy!' She shrugged helplessly.

On Monday morning, Kelly began to suspect that Matt was avoiding her. By Monday night, she was positive about it. On Tuesday evening after clinic, they had their monthly meeting to discuss the practice and hand out the new rosters. Bianca gave an overview of the budget and supplies that had come in. Once she'd finished her bit, she said goodnight to them, leaving them to discuss the more medical side, as well as their patients.

'I received a call from the audio testing department at Wangaratta hospital today,' Kelly told Matt. 'Justin's hearing is perfect.'

'Good. Natasha called me yesterday evening to say she'd met Lorraine and Justin without a problem.'

Kelly didn't miss the reference to Natasha calling him at home as that's where Matt would have been yesterday evening. She felt a twinge of jealousy shoot through her but managed to push it aside. 'I think we should get Lorraine in tomorrow because there are a few tests I'd like to do on Justin. Just simple, logical tests which will give us a good indication whether it is autism or not. Would you sit in on the consult again, Matt?'

He nodded.

'Poor little thing,' Rhea crooned. 'It's not going to be easy for Lorraine.'

'No, it's not. Do either of you know what type of support the Autism Association offers in Wangaratta?'

'I'll get onto it,' Matt replied and noted it down. 'I've received information regarding Abby and Carl. Carl has been discharged but has taken up my referral to get some counselling.'

'Good. And Abby?'

'The orthopaedic surgeon praised your work, saying he couldn't have done a better job himself and is extremely pleased with her progress. She'll be discharged to a re-habilitation hospital in Melbourne either tomorrow or Thursday.'

'Excellent.'

'Rhea, how's Bianca coping with her asthma in this wet weather?' Kelly asked. 'She sounded very wheezy yester-day.'

'I'm monitoring her closely and have asked her to take a few days off but she refuses. She says she won't let asthma rule her life and if she was going to have an attack, she'd rather have it here than at home.' Rhea shrugged. 'I must say, it seems logical to me.'

They talked for a while longer about a few other patients before Rhea said, 'Oh, Kelly, I haven't had a spare moment to ask you about Freddy. How did he take the news?'

Kelly shrugged. 'In typical Freddy fashion.' She was con-scious of the way Matt's back had straightened at the men-tion of her ex-husband. 'He ranted and raved for a while but finally accepted it as the truth.'

'Now what?' Matt asked.

'"Now what" what?' Kelly frowned at him.

'Does he want to marry you again? Become involved with the child?'

'I don't know.'

'What?' Matt didn't raise his voice but was clearly perplexed.

'He said he needed some time to think and he'd get back to me.'

'And that's it.'

'Well, he'll probably discuss it with his parents even though he told me he wouldn't. Freddy is completely incapable of making any decisions on his own so this is by no means over.'

'Why?' Rhea asked.

Kelly frowned. 'How can I explain this?' She thought for a moment. 'Freddy's family are…well, overbearing and domineering is the best way to describe his parents. They've been demanding that Freddy produce an heir to carry on the family name for quite a few years.'

'Only interested in boys.' Rhea nodded. 'I know their type.'

'His sister's already had three boys but that's not good enough. Producing an heir has become very important to Freddy. It was the main reason Freddy agreed to the divorce.'

'*You* asked for the divorce?' Matt was stunned. For some reason, he'd thought her ex had wanted the divorce.

'Yes. I could tell things weren't working and I didn't want to continue to the point where we hated each other.'

'And Freddy only agreed because the two of you couldn't have children and his parents were ordering him to give them male grandchildren?'

'Yes.'

'Sounds like a twisted family to me.'

'You have no idea *how* twisted,' Kelly replied with feeling.

'So you think his parents might make him file for custody?'

'Yes.' Kelly pulled the clip from her hair and fluffed her fingers through it. 'But I guess I'll cross that bridge when I come to it.'

'Does Freddy know you'd fight for custody?'

'Yes.'

'Kelly!'

'What?'

'You don't tell the enemy your plans,' Matt pointed out.

'I don't consider Freddy my enemy,' she said clearly. 'Look, Matt, all this is irrelevant until I hear from Freddy.'

'Which will be when?'

'I have no idea. If he hasn't called me by the end of the week, I'll give him a call.'

Matt crossed his arms defensively over his chest and clamped his jaw tight.

'It's not an easy decision for him to make,' Kelly defended. 'I urged him to try and make this one on his own, but if he doesn't have strong people around him, propping him up, he'll cave in and talk to his parents. I just hope this Carmen Ristoro is someone he can lean on.'

'Carmen Ristoro?' Rhea sat up straighter in her chair. Then she snapped her fingers. '*That's* where I've seen Freddy before. He was in the paper with Carmen Ristoro.'

Kelly nodded. 'He mentioned that. Who is she?'

'She's the daughter of the extremely wealthy Miguel Ristoro.'

'Who?' Matt and Kelly asked in unison.

'Oh, fair dinkum, you two. Where have you been hiding? Miguel Ristoro is a prominent businessman. Wheat and wool, that type of thing. He's involved with nearly everything exported from Australia.'

'And now Freddy's parents want him to marry her,' Kelly stated, as though it all made perfect sense.

Rhea nodded. 'It said in the paper that they'd been dating for quite some time and that there were rumours they'd be married before Christmas.'

'If they get married and then Freddy files for custody—' Matt broke off, and Kelly realised where he was going.

'The court would see that Freddy would be able to supply

a two-parent home as opposed to me, a single mother who moves every six months.'

'You need a husband,' Matt stated.

'And a stable one at that,' Rhea added.

'Whoa!' Kelly held up her hands to both of them. 'I don't need anything of the kind. The marriage might never even go ahead. Freddy told me he *liked* Carmen but wasn't sure about getting into another marriage that might fail.'

'Even so…' Matt stood and paced the room '…you'd have a stronger leg to stand on if you were settled in a permanent job.'

'Which allowed you time to care for your child,' Rhea added.

'And therefore showing you provided the best and most stable atmosphere for a child to be raised in.' Matt stopped pacing and raked one hand through his hair. He looked at Kelly before nodding slowly. 'There's only one thing to do.'

'What?' She couldn't look away. Couldn't break from his hypnotic gaze.

He shrugged, his expression dead serious. 'You'll have to marry me.'

CHAPTER EIGHT

'WH...UM...AH.' Kelly returned his gaze, transfixed by Matt and his proposal. For one split second she was tempted to accept. The natural chemistry between herself and Matt was explosive. What she felt for Matt surpassed her previous feelings for Freddy, and she'd married Freddy!

Could she?

She forced herself to break from his gaze and looked at Rhea. The other woman had her hands clutched to her chest in anxiousness, nodding furiously like those silly little toy dogs people had in the back windows of their cars.

Kelly looked back at Matt and knew she couldn't do this to him—or herself. Butterflies churned in her stomach and she was glad she was sitting down as she knew for a fact that her legs would have refused to support her.

'Matt.' Her throat was dry and she cleared her throat. 'There's only one problem.'

'What?' he asked, as though daring her to voice an objection. He couldn't be serious, but his expression told her otherwise.

'You don't love me.' She felt a pain shoot straight through her heart as she said the words. As Matt didn't instantly dispute the fact, she knew they were true. She swallowed over the lump which had appeared in her throat, Rhea's presence completely forgotten. 'A marriage between us would be fun for a while, but to do it simply to get at Freddy's family would be ridiculous.

'Besides,' she rushed on, 'all of what we're talking about is pure speculation. Freddy might not tell his parents. He might not marry Carmen. He might want to be a part of his child's life.'

Matt clenched his jaw and nodded. 'You're probably right.' He shrugged with indifference. 'The offer still stands if things go from bad to worse,' he stated matter-of-factly, before gathering up his papers from the table. 'Is there anything else we need to discuss?'

Rhea shook her head. 'Not that I can think of.'

'Fine.' He nodded, putting the papers into his briefcase. 'Then, if you ladies will excuse me, I'll head home and get started on my paperwork.'

''Night,' Rhea called.

Kelly forced a smile, still unable to believe what had just transpired. Matt had proposed to her! Matt—who she was irresistibly attracted to and who had woven magic in her dreams and her life ever since she'd arrived in Bright. He closed the door quietly behind him, leaving the two women alone. Kelly, though, had never felt more bereft in her life, and the sensation threw her.

'What did you do that for?' Rhea exploded the instant he was gone. 'Are you out of your mind?'

Kelly groaned and buried her head in her hands.

'You and Matt have something going for you,' Rhea stated.

She looked up at her friend. 'Sure, but do we love each other?' Kelly's words were soft. 'I've been in a marriage before, Rhea, where there was no love—real, deep, for ever love. I don't want to make the same mistakes again.'

'But I thought you and Freddy were friends?'

'That's true, but there's still a lot of heartache to deal with on the road to divorce. Amicable or not.'

'I guess.' Rhea leaned back in her chair. 'I must confess that I was very surprised by Matt's proposal.'

'*You* were! I'm still trembling.' She tried to laugh but it came out more as a half-sob.

'Really?' Rhea raised her eyebrows interestedly. 'Symptoms, Kelly. Think about those symptoms.'

Kelly waved her words away and cleared her throat. 'It was just surprise. It doesn't mean anything.'

'But aren't you interested in him? I know you've kissed.'

'So? That doesn't mean we have to get married. Matt is such a genuinely caring man, I guess it wasn't so out of character for him to do it. He's only thinking logically and he knows how much this baby means to me.'

'Why?'

Kelly looked surprised. 'Haven't I told you?' At Rhea's shake of the head, Kelly explained about her endometriosis.

'And Matt knows this?'

'Yes.'

'Well...I'd say you two are *definitely* more chummy than "just friends".'

'Why? "Just friends" can talk about all sorts of things together.'

'Really? Then how many other men, besides the doctors who have treated you, know about your condition?'

'My dad and Freddy.'

'And now Matt. You know, at first I couldn't figure you out, Kelly. You come across all self-assured and confident, but when you crack through that thick shell of yours, you're all gooey and soft inside.'

Kelly laughed. 'Thanks a lot. You make me sound like a hard-boiled egg.'

Rhea's laughter died away. 'In all seriousness, Kelly, how *are* you going to do it? Raise a child on your own? I have two children and although Joe works nights and we sometimes need to get a babysitter in, it's awfully hard work. And I usually have my parents here as well as Matt. It's not easy.'

'I never expected it to be, but we all adjust, Rhea. We all cope with what's handed to us.'

'Sure, but *if* things get too much, *will* you ask for help and if so, from *whom*? Your parents are overseas and you don't stay anywhere long enough to make lasting friendships.'

'I have lasting friendships, even if most of my friends do live overseas.' Kelly frowned, then sighed. 'Matt's asked me the same questions and, believe me, I'm working on the answers. I really am. I was thinking of taking the next six months off after this contract so I could have the baby and get settled into motherhood.'

'But where would that be?'

She shrugged her shoulders. 'Salzburg? Davos? London?'

'You're going to go overseas?'

'It will be easier to spend time with my parents if I need them,' Kelly admitted. 'Basing myself here in Australia will make it too hard for them to visit their only grandchild.'

'And do you think Freddy's going to let you take his child out of the country? His parents would most certainly put up a fight in that respect.'

'I know.' Kelly massaged her temples with her fingers. 'Honestly, Rhea. It just seems as though my entire world has flipped off its axis and I'm just spinning around in the galaxy, completely lost. I've never felt this way before but, then, I've always regarded myself as a person who likes a challenge so I'm trying to view this whole issue positively.'

'Well, I have a recommendation for you.'

'What?'

'Stay here.'

'But we've just been through that. I can't marry Matt.'

'You don't have to, although personally I think he'd be a bonus.'

Kelly looked down at her hands. 'What about Natasha?'

'Natasha?' Rhea was clearly puzzled. 'What's she got to do with this?'

Kelly cleared her throat and met Rhea's gaze again. 'I just thought…that, well, that she and Matt were…'

Rhea chuckled. 'You think there's something between Matt and Natasha,' she stated, but quickly shook her head. 'If that's what's been holding you back from throwing yourself at my brother, forget it. There's nothing between them. They're just friends. Trust me. Natasha's still carrying a torch for her first husband, and after what happened with Conrad I doubt she'll be rushing down the aisle again. But we're not here to discuss Natasha. You should stay here in Bright, Kelly.'

'Why?' Kelly felt as though a weight had been removed from her shoulders. There was nothing between Natasha and Matt! She hadn't realised it had bothered her so much.

'Why?' Rhea repeated. 'Because you fit in, but if you want logical reasons, then consider this. You could rent a place for twelve months and I could deliver your baby. You could work part time here at the clinic and you wouldn't even need to do hospital rotations or anything like that, which would take you away from the baby at odd hours. Most of all, you'd have support. My mother would be thrilled to have another baby to fuss over and it would take the pressure off her asking me when I'm going to have number three.'

'When are you?' Kelly couldn't resist asking, hoping to take the spotlight off herself for a moment.

'Maybe sooner than you think.'

Kelly sat up. 'You're not?'

'No, but Joe and I are talking about a third so that would also give your baby a little playmate. Go on, Kelly. It makes perfect sense. You're not too far away from Melbourne and that way Freddy can visit whenever he wants.'

Kelly was silent while she considered Rhea's words. She closed her eyes and shook her head. 'And what about Matt?'

'What about him?'

'Well, for starters, how would he feel if I accepted your offer? You haven't discussed this with him, or your father, and they are both partners in this clinic.'

'Oh, neither of them will object and we do need another doctor, even when Dad returns. He'll be working part time and gradually easing off into full-time retirement, so it all works out perfectly.' Rhea clapped her hands with glee. 'Come on, Kelly. At least think it over.'

Kelly laughed. 'You're like a bulldozer, Rhea. All right. I'll think it over but I'll also be talking it over with Matt. Another thing to consider is the distance the baby will be from my parents.'

'Trust me, honey. Where there are grandchildren involved, grandparents will travel to the ends of the earth. They'll do anything for them.'

'That's reassuring to know regarding *my* parents, but *not* Freddy's.'

'You can't have it all.' Rhea held her hands out wide. 'Listen, how about coming over for dinner? Joe should be putting the finishing touches to the meal and, trust me, not only is he a great husband and father but he's an excellent cook.'

'Sounds great.'

They locked up the clinic and headed across the road to Rhea's house. Kelly couldn't help glancing over at Matt's. Was he regretting having proposed to her? Was he disappointed that she hadn't accepted? Because right at this moment, the idea of accepting was far too tempting.

'Come on in, Lorraine. Good morning, Justin.' Kelly showed her patients in. She knew Bianca would have buzzed through to Matt when Lorraine and Justin had arrived, yet Kelly couldn't help glancing around the corridor, hoping to see him.

He'd been as elusive and as slippery as a bar of soap in

a bathtub of water. She wasn't even sure if he was here this morning. She wasn't sure whether to wait for him or not, but if he'd been held up with a patient, it could take a while.

'Do you have the results of the hearing test?' Lorraine asked a little anxiously.

'Yes. I'm sure they told you on the day that Justin's hearing was fine?'

'Yes, but I wasn't sure whether they were just saying that so I wouldn't worry or whether something was really wrong.'

'No. He passed with flying colours.'

'They were talking in whispers all the time. Whispering things to each other and then looking at me in a worried way. It really freaked me out.'

Kelly smiled. 'Some medical professionals are just like that.' She handed the test results to Lorraine. 'See for yourself.'

Lorraine scanned the sheet before nodding. 'Well, that's good to know.'

'Yes, it is. How have you both been sleeping?'

'Yeah, really great. I did what you suggested and gave him a bottle at the same time I gave him that medicine those nights, and it's worked. He's still sleeping in my bed but at least we're sleeping.'

'That's the important thing at this stage.' There was a brief knock on her door and Matt came in a second later. He was dressed in a dark grey suit and the colour seemed to match the scowl on his face when he glanced at Kelly— dark and brooding.

'Sorry I'm late.' He placed a manila folder on Kelly's desk.

'Not at all. Lorraine was just telling me that they've settled into a better sleeping routine.'

'Excellent,' Matt praised. 'I presume everything went smoothly at the hospital? You met Natasha all right?'

'She's lovely. She stayed with us the entire time and even took us out to lunch afterwards.'

'That's Natasha. She's a very giving person.'

Kelly watched the way Matt's eyes lit up when he spoke about Natasha. Could Rhea have been wrong? Oh, let it go, she told herself sternly. Matt wasn't the type of man to make a pass at her if he was interested in someone else. Now *that* was something firm for her to believe in. Even though she'd only known him a short time, he was definitely a man of his word.

'So what's next, Kelly?' Lorraine's words brought her back to reality. 'All the tests so far have shown him to be fine.'

'How many of his toy cars do you have with you today?' Kelly asked, and Lorraine immediately started digging around in the big baby bag she carried around with her and started pulling out toy cars.

Kelly counted them. 'Seven, eight, nine. Good. If you could just put them on the floor in front of Justin, that would be good.'

Lorraine did so and sat back. 'What exactly are you looking for?' she asked.

'You said he was lining his toys up, rather than playing with them.'

'That's right.'

'I'd just like to see *how* he does it.'

'It's quite amazing, really. First he sorts them by colour and shape and puts them in a pattern. Quite bright, I've always thought.'

'He *is* an extremely smart little boy,' Matt said.

They watched as Justin played with his favourite car for a few minutes then put it down. He then started 'adding' to that car. Yellow, then green, then blue. Some cars were the same colour and others were the same shape and one was two-toned.

He continued to line them up and Kelly tried to gues which one came next in the sequence. Which one matchec in shape or colour? When he came to the two-toned car, he became frustrated and shoved the cars away, sending them flying in all directions.

'That's what usually happens,' Lorraine said.

Matt collected the cars and gave them to him again. He went through the motions, doing everything in exactly the same way as before. Again he got frustrated and shoved the cars away. Matt collected them again but this time he kept Justin's favourite car, as well as the two-toned one.

Justin looked at the cars before starting to search. He patted Lorraine's bag but still didn't make eye contact with her.

'Here they are, Justin,' Matt said, and held them out. Justin took his favourite car but left the two-toned one before sitting down and concentrating on his puzzle again. This time, he didn't become frustrated.

Kelly met Matt's gaze and he nodded. It was time they told Lorraine about their suspicions.

'Autism?' Lorraine said a few minutes later. 'What's that?'

'It's a disorder of higher brain function. That means there are certain pathways within the brain that don't correspond properly. Usually children with autism are withdrawn, self-absorbed and are unable to communicate by normal speech.'

Lorraine clamped her hand over her mouth and tears started to brim in her eyes. 'Is he going to be all right?'

'Physically, he's fine,' Kelly said.

'Mentally, he's not,' Matt finished.

'How long have you suspected he had this autism thing?'

'From the first consult,' Kelly explained softly. 'When he was sitting down, rocking slightly, and also when he didn't make eye contact. They're classic signs, but I wanted to be absolutely sure first, which is why we needed an EEG, which would rule out epilepsy, and also the hearing test, which ruled out deafness.'

Lorraine covered her face with both her hands and started to cry. Matt leaned over and placed his arm around her shoulders. Kelly handed Lorraine tissues and checked on Justin who hadn't bothered to raise his head at the disruption.

'This means…I'm a…' Lorraine hiccuped '…good mother.'

'You'd better believe you are,' Kelly said firmly. 'There's nothing wrong with your parenting skills.'

'That's nice to hear but when he won't sit down to eat or he doesn't say "Ta" when I hand him something or any of the normal things, people think I'm a bad mother and I'm not disciplining my child.'

'Well, they're very wrong,' Matt soothed. Lorraine cried for a bit longer before wiping her eyes and blowing her nose.

'What happens next?'

'We'd like you to contact the Autism Association.' Matt picked the manila folder off Kelly's desk and opened it, handing Lorraine the information. 'I've included a referral letter for you to give them. As you can see by the list, the Melbourne branch of the association offers quite a few services in Wangaratta.' They went through the information, with Matt explaining what each section was responsible for. He also outlined the government benefits and support she'd be eligible to receive.

'So there's something wrong with his brain, but how do I fix it? I mean, I know I can't fix it, but how do I talk to him? Communicate?'

'Good question.' Kelly nodded. 'I think the easiest way to describe it is to use a computer as an analogy. With a computer, it only knows what the programmer puts in. If the programming remains the same, everything runs smoothly. If a computer virus enters the system, then things start to go wrong.

'Justin needs programming, and for a while things will run smoothly for you, but he's a living, breathing person, not an inanimate object. His body will change. His needs will change and each time he needs to be reprogrammed. That's where the Autism Association can help. They have methods and ways of helping with that programming.

'Remember, Lorraine, that we're here with you every step of the way,' Kelly encouraged. 'If you have any questions, call us. If you're concerned about Justin in any way, call us.'

'There are parent support groups as well,' Matt added, 'where other mothers might be able to offer helpful suggestions and also they understand what you're going through.'

'But the next thing we need to do is to get Justin graded. As Matt's already explained, there are several levels of autism and a lot of autistic people fall into the category of genius.'

'That's right. Don't think because they have something wrong with their brain that they're not smart. Lining those cars up in a colour-coded pattern is something beyond a normal eighteen-month-old child,' he pointed out. 'But we need to know at what level Justin is. In other words, how autistic he is.'

Lorraine nodded.

'This is all rather a lot to take in, I know, but read the information Matt's given you and let either one of us know if you have any further questions.'

'All right,' Lorraine replied, and blew her nose once more. She stood and started collecting the cars, making sure Justin still had his favourite one. Matt quickly bent to help her. When she'd gathered her belongings together she spoke to Justin. 'How about you and Mummy go and get an ice cream?' she asked him.

He didn't move. He didn't look at her.

'Justin?' She reached for his hand but he tugged it away. 'He does this sometimes,' she explained to Matt and Kelly, obviously a little embarrassed.

'You're not saying the right words,' Kelly pointed out softly.

'What do you mean? What words should I be saying?'

'Every time you've left somewhere, you've always said, "Come on, Justin. Home time." Try it now.'

Lorraine looked at Matt who nodded encouragingly. 'Come on, Justin. Home time.' The instant the words were out of her mouth, Justin stood and toddled over to her side, his favourite car still in his hands, not looking at anyone.

'It's all about commands and programming,' Kelly repeated. She could tell Lorraine was dazed. 'You'll do fine,' she encouraged.

Lorraine nodded her head quickly, her bottom lip quivering as she took one of Justin's hands in hers. 'Thanks.'

Matt held the door open for them.

'Did you want to see us again?' Lorraine asked Kelly.

'Only if you want to. I'm here to talk and help you understand and so is Matt, but medically, no. Contact the Autism Association and let us know what happens.'

'All right and…thanks.'

Kelly watched her go before sitting down in her chair and covering her face with her hands. What if something like that happened to her child? What if he or she was born with a disability? She'd be a single parent, struggling to cope. She might even have to give up medicine for a few years and then she'd have trouble getting a job.

'There's a lot to think about.' At the sound of his voice she quickly lifted her head.

'Sorry. I thought you'd gone.'

'No such luck.' Matt closed the door and walked towards her. 'I'd like to talk to you if that's all right.' He looked at his watch. 'We've both got about five minutes before our next patients arrive.'

Kelly took a deep breath and forced a smile. 'Sure.' Was it just her or did he feel uneasy as well? That proposal last night had changed the atmosphere between them, and she wasn't sure whether they'd be able to get it back onto a more even footing. One where she could flirt with him but not have it taken seriously.

'After I left last night, I did a lot of thinking and I wanted to apologise if I put you in an uncomfortable position.'

'Matt, it's—'

He held up his hand to stop her. 'Please.' He paced around in front of her desk and then stopped, raking a hand through his hair. 'I've never proposed to any one before but what you were saying—' He broke off and looked at her. 'Kelly, I know how much this baby means to you. I understand that and I think you need to do everything you can to give it the best start in life.'

He started pacing again. 'But I've realised that whatever you decide to do, this is *your* baby. I have no say in what you do but I hope you'll listen to the advice I've already given you. Raising a child on your own, well, it can't be easy and…' He stopped and planted his hands on his hips, shaking his head. 'I usually pride myself on being an articulate man but…' he laughed '…I don't seem to be doing a very good job of explaining myself.'

'You certainly surprised your sister, not to mention me, with your proposal.' Kelly laughed nervously.

'Hmm.' He looked down at her lips, his gaze hovering for a few seconds too long. It was enough to change the atmosphere between them, especially when he flicked his gaze back to her eyes and she saw raw desire burning within the blue depths.

In an effort to lighten the mood, she raised her eyebrows teasingly. 'Although…' she slowly stood, her hand sliding up his arm to his shoulder before she caressed the back of his neck and let her fingers play in the ends of his hair '…I was *very* tempted to say yes.' Their faces were millimetres apart and she saw him swallow convulsively. 'If only to see where this attraction would lead us.'

Matt edged back onto the desk and in one swift movement opened his legs and pulled her closer to him. His hands were on her waist, holding her captive. Their breath mingled together and she knew their hearts were tattooing the same rhythm.

The pretence was gone and again Kelly wondered how things had happened so fast. When he slid his hands up her back, bringing her chest into contact with his, all mischief, all teasing left her in a rush.

This was real. This was Matt. This was…amazing. How did this man make her feel so completely out of control?

'What would happen if we gave in to temptation?' he murmured, as his head edged marginally closer to hers. 'Where would that leave us?'

For a moment, she couldn't speak. Her mouth was dry and she wet her lips in anticipation. Her heart pounded against her ribs and the tension that filled her body screamed out for release. She swallowed. 'Kiss me, Matt,' she pleaded, and closed her eyes, unable to bear the sweet torture.

'I swore to myself that I was going to leave you alone. You don't need me in your life as a complication, and I certainly don't need you complicating mine either.'

'Shh.' She didn't want to focus on logic. She wanted to focus on feeling. It seemed to be the only time she was *really* happy—when she was in Matt's arms, being swept away on a tide of passion and intrigue. 'Kiss me,' she urged again.

She could feel the battle within him, feel the push-pull of his emotions. His body definitely wanted her, of that much she was absolutely certain, but his mind was powerful and although she respected it, this time around she wanted the mind to keep quiet.

'I want you, Kelly.' Matt touched his cheek to hers and she gasped at the contact.

With that, he finally angled his head towards her waiting mouth, and when they eventually touched, Kelly felt her own lips tremble with relief. She sighed into the kiss, feeling the tension burst and evaporate, only to be replaced by a mass of uncontrollable tinglings. Leaning against him, she wound her arms possessively about his neck, loving the feel of their bodies so close together.

This was right. This was where they both belonged, Kelly thought, but quickly dismissed the notion as impossible. Matt was just someone she was fiercely attracted to. This couldn't be love. This couldn't possibly be the real thing. Surely it didn't happen *this* quickly?

With the reverberation of her heartbeat pounding in her ears, she gave herself up to the hot and hungry demands of his mouth, following his lead and matching his intensity. Was this *another* goodbye kiss? If it was, she could get used to them.

Her consulting-room door opened and Rhea poked her head around. 'Bianca's having an asthma attack.' In the next second, she was gone.

Kelly and Matt sprang instantly apart, like children being caught by their parents. They stared at each other for a split second before Rhea's words started to sink in. They both rushed out to the reception area to help. There was only one other person in the waiting room and Kelly was thankful that it wasn't full of anxious spectators.

Rhea was crouched down beside Bianca's seat, pulling a nebuliser mask from its container. 'Matt, salbutamol, stat,' she ordered. 'Kelly, do her obs.'

'Acknowledged.' Kelly reached for the medical kit they

kept stocked at the receptionist's desk for emergencies such
as this. She wrapped the BP cuff around Bianca's arm, noticing how pale and clammy her skin was. 'BP is one-sixty
over one-twenty. Pulse is one-fifty. Lips are blue. Bianca,
do you have a stabbing pain around your ribs?' Bianca nodded. 'Costochondritis.'

'Ibuprofen,' Rhea ordered firmly. 'That will help decrease
that pain, Bianca,' she explained. The nebuliser was hooked
up and after everyone encouraged Bianca to breathe nor-
mally, the colour started returning to her lips as well as her
face.

'Keep breathing,' Rhea said and patted the receptionist's
shoulder. 'You're doing fine. All right, everyone, crisis
averted. Everything's under control. I'll stay with her. You
two can get back to what you were doing—er, I mean, get
back to your patients,' Rhea corrected with a cheeky grin.

Kelly laughed and Matt frowned at his sister before picking up a set of case-notes and calling his patient through.
Kelly looked at her list and as the waiting room was empty
concluded her patient hadn't arrived yet.

'So what was that all about?' Rhea asked softly, her back
to Kelly as she monitored Bianca.

'Would you like a cup of tea, Rhea? Coffee?'

Rhea laughed. 'Have you changed your mind, just like
you're trying to change the subject?'

'No. I haven't changed my mind.'

'I'll have a tea,' Rhea said. 'And bring a glass of water
for Bianca.'

'Will do,' Kelly said, glad to get away from Rhea's pry-
ing questions. She wasn't sure whether Matt wanted a cuppa
or not but although he probably didn't want to see her just
now, she decided to make him one anyway. She wasn't a
coward. She wasn't going to deny she'd just begged him to
kiss her. They'd both enjoyed it—far too much. That was
the problem.

Rhea's suggestion that she stay in Bright spun around in her head. It would certainly tie everything together. She'd be able to work, raise her child and see where this relationship with Matt was going to end up.

'No.' She spooned sugar into her cup and then tossed the spoon into the sink, along with the tea. What was she doing? She didn't *take* sugar. This whole situation with Matt was starting to send her around the twist. She couldn't stop thinking about him. She couldn't stop wondering what he would think about the decisions she was making. His opinion mattered far too much to her and that in itself was odd.

The only opinions which had ever really mattered to her in the past had been those of her parents. Those two people who were so incredible at their jobs, at giving to people, of being there when people needed them.

Were they there for *her*? Had they ever really been there for her? When she'd told them she was marrying Freddy, they hadn't quizzed her about him but had accepted her decision. They supported her, yes, but were they *there* for her?

All her life, they'd been helping others. Sure, she'd learnt a lot and had grown up very quickly. Perhaps that was why she tended to act a little childishly sometimes—because her own childhood hadn't been a normal one.

Kelly shook her head. Where had she got the notion that she had to travel the globe, like her parents, to help people out? She'd had a fantastic time doing it, but wasn't it about time she started helping herself? She had another life to think about now—a very important life and one that would change hers for ever.

She needed to talk to Matt to ask his opinion on Rhea's idea, because the more she thought about it, the more she wanted to stay here in Bright. She carried the tea and water out to the reception area and was pleased to see Bianca looking more like her relaxed and cheerful self.

'I've called her husband and he's coming to pick her up.'

'I'm OK,' Bianca said from behind the mask.

'You're going home,' Rhea stated firmly. 'We're almost done here and I'm sure Kelly, Matt and I won't destroy your patient record and filing system too much.'

Bianca smiled. 'All right, then.'

Rhea turned to Kelly. 'She says that like she has some say in it.' They all laughed.

'I'll just take Matt's tea into him.' Kelly headed back to the kitchen. She smiled as she stirred the sugar in, amazed she felt excited about seeing him again. It was ridiculous.

She carried the tea and knocked on his door. She waited for him to call her in, not wanting to barge in when he was with a patient. Kelly entered and when she saw him sitting behind his desk, looking expectantly at her, her step faltered and she spilled some of the liquid over her hand.

She didn't feel it.

'Are you all right, Kelly?' He came around his desk to take the cup from her.

'Uh... Hmm.' She couldn't pull her gaze away from him as one sensation after another swamped her completely.

They were compelling. They were frightening and they were very, very real.

Without another word, she spun around and all but bolted out the door. She raced back to her own consulting room and sat down in her chair, feet up on the desk, and pressed her fingers to the pounding pulse at her wrist.

This wasn't happening. It *couldn't* be happening.

If she was reading her symptoms correctly, she was in love with Matt!

CHAPTER NINE

'IMPOSSIBLE!' Kelly breathed.

Seconds later, her door opened and she sprang upright in her chair. Matt burst in, concern written all over his face.

'Are you all right?' He came over and placed his hand on her forehead. Kelly wished he wouldn't stand so close, especially as he smelt so good. She stood up, effectively breaking the contact and forcing Matt to take a step away.

'I'm fine.'

'You went so pale when you came into my room just now. Are you sure? Is the baby all right? Do you have any pain?'

'I'm fine, Matt,' she reiterated. 'The baby's fine. I don't have any pain... I just get a little exhausted near the end of the day. Nothing I can't handle.'

'We can cancel your last few patients.'

'No. They won't take long.'

'Promise me you'll rest and relax when you get home.'

'I promise,' she said, and closed her eyes in disbelief at the way her voice had turned all husky and seductive. Why did it do that without her permission? She opened her eyes and cleared her throat. 'Go.' She urged. 'You have a patient waiting and...er...as Bianca's getting ready to go home, I'd better check the waiting room for my next patient.'

'Are you *sure* you're all right?'

'Yes.'

'You're not just being brave?'

'Matt, if there was something wrong with the baby, I promise you'll be one of the first to know.'

He raked a hand through his hair and nodded, as though

accepting her answer. 'I'll check on you later,' he told her as he turned and walked out of the room.

Kelly sighed with relief when he'd gone and headed to the waiting room. Her patient had arrived so she called her in. An hour later, Kelly was ready to call through her last patient for the day.

'Jana?' she said in surprise when she checked the waiting room. 'Hi. What brings you here?'

'I…I've made an appointment to see you. A quarter to five it was for?'

Kelly looked at the clock on the wall and, seeing as it read a quarter *past* five, quickly apologised. She picked up Jana's file. 'Come on through.' Once they were settled in her consulting room, Kelly smiled at the other woman. 'What can I do for you today?'

'Well, I wanted to see you because I feel a little uncomfortable seeing either Rhea or Matt—you know, because of my history with Matt.'

Kelly nodded understandingly.

'I've been trying to decide whether to leave the mountain or not,' Jana explained. 'I've been talking about it for years but now a real opportunity has come up and I don't think I can pass this one up.' She explained a bit more about what was going on and Kelly listened patiently. 'It's just that every time something like this happens, I start to have…well…things go wrong.'

'Such as?'

'Well, my periods go all irregular and really painful and I get pains in my chest. I have ulcers in my mouth and I seem to have a constant headache.'

'Anxiety.'

'Anxiety?'

'Yes.' Kelly smiled. 'This is a big change for you. You were raised in this valley and it's clear how much you love it. Although this new job may take you down a different path, the decision whether or not to step outside your comfort zone is a hard one to make. Your body is reacting due to the amount of stress you're feeling. This stress is making you anxious.'

'What can I do?'

'There are several things you could do. First of all, make a list of pros and cons. Don't think staying here is the coward's way out. You have to do what's right for you and, don't forget, you can always come back here. Mount Buffalo isn't going to go anywhere.

'For your physical symptoms, try some manuka honey for your mouth ulcers. It works a treat. You can purchase it at the health food store but just make sure it's pure—that it hasn't been heated. The thicker the honey is, the more natural it is and the greater its healing properties. Root ginger is very good for period pain and also for helping to reduce stress. Evening primrose oil is good, too, and can be purchased from the chemist. With the ginger, again make sure it's the natural variety rather than the crystallised form. Chop it up finely or grate it and then pour boiling water over it to make a drink. Let it cool, sweeten it with honey or even add a bit of lemon.'

Jana frowned at her. 'You're really into all this natural stuff, aren't you?'

'Nature has been providing the answers to a lot of our problems for years. I'm not against antibiotics or other drugs widely used in medicine but natural remedies can often have a more soothing effect on our bodies.'

'What about my headaches?'

Kelly smiled and stood up, coming around to the back of Jana's chair. 'Do you have one now?'

'Yes.'

'All right. Sit still. I'm going to give you a bit of a shoulder rub.' While she gently massaged the knots in Jana's shoulders, Kelly asked her what she loved most about work-

ing at Mount Buffalo. As Jana talked, Kelly could feel the
other woman unwinding, and ten minutes later she returned
to her seat.

'How does that feel?'

'Tingly.' Jana laughed.

'And the headache?'

Jana thought for a moment. 'Gone!' she said in surprise.

'Tension, stress and anxiety. They're all closely related
but we need to look at the cause. Some people need medication to control their anxiety because its cause isn't something that will go away—like cancer patients, for example.'
Kelly wrote down the list of things for Jana to buy. 'Try
these. They're a lot less expensive as well. If you feel things
haven't changed in about seven days, come back and see
me again.'

'For another massage?' Jana moved her neck smoothly
from side to side.

Kelly laughed. 'Not just for that. There's bound to be
someone around these parts who gives good massages.'

'Yes.' Jana nodded and named a woman who lived just
outside Bright. 'I'll book myself in today.'

'Good.' Kelly handed Jana the list.

'Thanks, Kelly. I'm really glad I came to talk to you.
You're completely different from how I'd thought you'd
be.'

Kelly laughed. 'Gee, thanks.'

'You know what I mean. The fact that you're dating
Matt.'

Now it was Kelly's turn to be surprised. 'I'm not dating
Matt.'

'Really? Then you must be very interested in each other.
The way the two of you were gazing into each other's eyes
at the weekend made everyone there take notice.'

'Oh' was all Kelly could think of to say. She walked with
Jana to the door. 'Let me know how it goes.'

'I will, and all the best with Matt. I think you're just wha
he needs.'

Kelly was glad to finally get home that night.

That day she'd discovered something she'd though
would never happen—she'd fallen in love. Not only that
but she'd fallen in love with a man who classified her as
complication. Then one of his ex-girlfriends had said tha
she was just what he needed. Not that she cared what othe
people thought, but in some ways it was nice to get Jana'
approval—after all, she'd known Matt since high school.

She sighed as she lay down on the couch and sipped he
cup of peppermint tea, closing her eyes. Since she'd set foc
in Bright, her life had changed. Even though she hadn'
known about the baby, her life had still changed. Sh
thought back to when she'd first looked at Matt from be
neath her helmet visor and realised it was then that her emo
tions had started to go haywire.

'And what a ride it's been,' she murmured. The phon
rang and she groaned, getting off the couch to answer i
wishing for a cordless phone. 'Hello. Dr O'Shea.'

'Kel.' Freddy's voice came down the other end. Kell
settled herself on the floor, leaning up against the wall, he
cup of tea beside her.

'How's it going, Freddy?' Hopefully, this would be i
Freddy would give her the information she needed so sh
could start planning the rest of her life!

'Ah…better. Better than the last time I saw you at an
rate. How are you feeling?'

'I'm fine.'

'And our baby?'

Our baby! That was a good start. 'The baby's fine, too.

'All right. I know you don't like to beat about the bus
so I'll let you know my decision.'

'I'd appreciate it.'

'I want to be involved in the baby's life.'

'Good.' She kept her tone bland whilst inside it was screaming with caution. 'Have you told your parents?'

'Ah…yes.'

Kelly closed her eyes in anguish. Saddle up, she thought. 'What did they say?'

'They didn't believe me and have demanded paternity tests. They said this was just the sort of thing you'd do to get your hands on the family's money.'

'I see they haven't changed.'

'I told them that you don't lie and I believed you without having a paternity test. You'd think as doctors they'd understand that tests like that to an unborn child could have drastic consequences. Besides, as far as I'm concerned, your word is as good as the truth.'

'Thank you, Freddy.' She opened her eyes and sighed before picking up the cup and taking a sip of the soothing liquid inside.

'You've never lied to me, Kel, and you wouldn't start now.'

'Thank you,' she repeated.

'I told my parents I wanted to be a part of the baby's life and was surprised when they insisted on it. They want to push forward the wedding with Carmen.' He sounded so confused Kelly took pity on him.

'Is that what *you* want, Freddy?'

'I don't know.'

'Do you love Carmen?'

'I don't know. It's happening way too fast.'

'Have you told Carmen about the baby?'

'No. My parents said not to tell her.'

'Freddy—I've said this before and I'll say it again. Why don't you think your parents ever liked me?'

'Because they didn't choose you.'

'Yes. Why else?'

'Because I listened to you.'

'Exactly. So listen to this, Freddy. You need to make up your own mind. You don't need to do everything your parents say. You're almost thirty-one and you're more than able to make decisions on your own. Trust yourself, Freddy. Trust your own judgement. Do you think it's wrong not to tell Carmen?'

'Actually, I do. She'd be a stepmother to our child—' the word made Kelly cringe '—and she has a right to know before she accepts a marriage proposal from me.'

'Then the next thing you should do is to talk to Carmen. What kind of hope would you have if your married life began with deceit? We had problems in our marriage, Freddy, but dishonesty was never one of them and things would definitely have been a lot harder if it had been.'

'So why don't I marry you again?'

'Freddy, don't joke.'

'I'm serious, Kel. Why don't we give it another go? We always wanted children and thought it would never happen. Now it is. I may not love you in that husband-wife kind of way but I do love you, Kel. More than that, I respect you.'

'Freddy, I—'

'It makes sense, honey. We'd be together, with *our* baby. You could move to Melbourne and we could live happily ever after.'

'Where?'

'Well, here. At my parents' house. You know how huge it is. I've got a whole wing to myself so there would be plenty of room for all of us.'

'Can you really see your parents and I living under the same roof?'

'You wouldn't even have to see them if you didn't want to.'

'And what about work? Where would I work, Freddy?' As if she didn't already know what he was going to say!

'In the family clinic. That's if you *wanted* to work. Mum gave up work when she had Francie and myself and then went back to it years later when I was at boarding school.'

'That's another thing. Our child is *not* going to boarding school.'

'But it's a tradition. Mum and Dad would be happy to pay for his tuition.'

'What if it's a girl?'

He stopped then. 'It wouldn't matter to me.'

'Would it matter to your parents? Come on, Freddy. They don't classify your sister's boys as true heirs. What if this baby is a girl? It's not as though I'm going to be able to get pregnant again at the drop of a hat. This might be a one-time thing.'

'Well, you got pregnant this time. Surely that's a good sign. Besides, we can do IVF and stuff like that.'

Kelly sighed heavily. 'Freddy, I don't think the two of us getting married again is a good idea.'

'Aw, come on, Kel. At least give it some thought.'

'I'm being honest with you. I don't love you, not in *that* way, just as you don't love me in *that* way. You've said so yourself.'

'But, Kel—'

'I don't need to think it over, Freddy, and I'm also not going to give you false hope by letting you think I might come around. I won't. I'm more than happy for *you* to be a part of the baby's life, but beyond that we'll just have to work it out.'

'Is there someone else?'

'What?'

'That Matt guy. Are you and he an item?'

'No,' she answered truthfully. 'Listen, Freddy. It's been a hectic day and I'm really tired. You go and talk to Carmen and call me in a few days to let me know what she says.'

'All right,' he said dejectedly. 'Take care of yourself and *our* baby.'

'I will. Bye.' She thankfully replaced the receiver and slumped down onto the floor whimpering at the way the problems in her life seemed to double in size within seconds.

Matt was concerned. He'd tried calling Kelly's number only to find it engaged. Who was she talking to? He'd been getting the engaged signal for almost two hours now and although he knew women could talk, *who* could she possibly be talking to for so long?

Freddy? Did they really have that much to say to each other? He supposed they did, but over two hours! Maybe she was talking to her mother, but as her parents were overseas the phone bill would be enormous.

Perhaps she'd fallen down and knocked the phone off the hook. Was she unconscious? Was the baby all right?

He had surprised himself with the level of protectiveness he felt towards her unborn child and had told himself over and over again that it was because of her endometriosis. He understood what it had meant that she'd finally conceived, but if he sat down and acknowledged the truth, his protectiveness wasn't for those reasons alone.

It was because Kelly had become far too important to him. Even though his proposal the other night had been made purely from a logical point of view, if she *had* accepted, he would have been extremely happy.

'Whoa!' He stood still, unable to believe his thoughts. 'Happy? With Kelly?'

He shook his head and concentrated on the task at hand. He tried her number again. Still engaged. Picking up a ring full of keys, he stormed out the door, heading for his parents' house. He turned the ancient doorbell, listening for the trilling sound it made. No answer.

Fitting the key into the lock, he opened the door.

'Kelly!' He saw her lying on the floor in the hallway and rushed to her side, knocking over a cup of tea in the process. He didn't care. 'Kelly,' he called more firmly, running his hands expertly over her body, feeling for breaks.

'Matt.' His name was a sigh on her lips and she reached up to cup his face. He couldn't feel any broken bones and he sagged onto the floor beside her with relief, narrowly missing the wet patch from the tea. He gathered her onto his lap.

'Are you all right, sweetheart?'

She snuggled into him. 'Hmm.'

'Kelly? Did you hurt yourself?'

'What?' She dragged herself from the depths of slumber and looked up at him. She blinked several times and when she tried to sit up straighter he tightened his grip on her.

'Just relax. You may have hurt yourself when you fell.'

'Fell? I didn't fall.'

'You were lying on the floor.'

'I was tired.' She wriggled a little then decided not to fight it. She was in Matt's arms. Where she wanted to be.

'You were tired? What, so you just lay down in the middle of the hallway and took a nap?'

'I guess so. I was on the phone.'

'I know. I've been trying to call you for the past two hours.'

'Two hours?' That made her sit up. Matt helped her to her feet and she noticed she hadn't replaced the receiver properly. 'Oops.' She looked at the phone.

'What?'

She smiled and put a hand over her mouth. 'I was talking to Freddy and I didn't hang up properly.' She shifted the receiver so it sat properly in the cradle before taking a step forward…and feeling instantly faint.

'Dizzy?'

'Yes.'

'Come and sit down,' he said, ushering her back to the lounge room. 'I'll make us some fresh tea.'

While Kelly waited, Matt cleaned up the spill and made them both a cuppa. 'Here you go,' he said, coming in and sitting down opposite her. 'Feeling better?'

'Yes. Thank you.' She took a sip of her tea, looking at him over the rim of her cup. 'My knight in shining armour.'

He didn't return her smile. 'So, what did Freddy decide?'

Kelly shook her head. 'He's a nutter.'

'So you've said before.'

'He wants to be involved in the baby's life.'

'That's good.'

'He's told his parents and they want a paternity test to prove it's his.'

'But that could harm the baby.'

'Yeah. You think they'd know that, seeing as they're doctors.'

Matt placed his cup on the table and started pacing the room. Kelly knew by now that when he did that he was agitated and needed to move to think things through. 'What else did Freddy say?'

'He suggested we remarry.'

'What?' He exploded.

Kelly was surprised at his reaction. Usually Matt took everything in his stride, but from the look on his face she guessed this was an exception to the rule. His hands were balled into fists and his eyes bored right into her. 'Tell me this is a joke, Kelly. Tell me you're pulling my leg.'

'I'm not, Matt. Freddy suggested we remarry.' She shrugged. 'You've got to admit it would make a lot of sense.'

'*What?*' His frown increased. 'You can't seriously be considering his offer.'

'Can't I?'

'No.'

'Why?'

'Because it's insane, that's why. He's completely wrong for you.'

'And you know this…how?'

'I met the guy.'

'You met him for five seconds, Matt. I was married to him for five years. I think I know Freddy a bit better than you do.'

Matt paced the floor again, calming himself down. 'You just can't marry him.'

'Why?' she pushed. All she wanted was for Matt to admit he loved her. He was willing to marry her, help with the baby, but was he willing to risk his heart and love her?

'If it's security you want for the baby, why didn't you accept me?'

Kelly shook her head and put her cup down before her trembling hands spilt the hot liquid. 'You just don't get it, do you, Matt? It's not the security I'm worried about. In this day and age, the world is scattered with single parents raising children. I can provide for the baby, financially and emotionally. I can also do it without giving up my career. Security isn't what I'm looking for, Matt.'

He stopped moving and stared at her. 'Then what *are* you looking for, Kelly? Because I can tell you right now, you won't find it with your ex-husband. He's all wrong for you.'

'Then who's right? Huh, Matt? Who's right for me?'

Their gazes held for a long moment and she silently willed him to say it. To say the words that would make everything all right. To say the words that would solve the heartache she was feeling. To say the words that would unite them for ever.

Instead, he threw his hands up in the air. 'How should I know who's right for you? You're…an enigma, Kelly. Ever since we met I've been trying to figure you out and it all becomes too confusing. You're sassy and confident one minute and the next you're like a young, innocent girl. You're gorgeous and sexy in everything you wear, whether it's green theatre scrubs or a ski-suit.' He raked his hand through his hair. 'You're giving and kind to others, wanting to help them with their problems, but when it comes to your own, you're too stubborn to ask for help. You've become involved in the community here yet you're more than happy to get up and leave at the end of six months. You like to roam around, never putting down roots or stepping outside your comfort zone, and all of this brings me back to square one to say I have no idea who would be right for you. But I know it's not Holdsworthy.'

Kelly dragged in a deep breath. 'I see.' She nodded a few times, willing away the tears that threatened to spill over. 'I see.' She sighed. 'I think you'd better go, Matt.'

'Kelly, I—'

'Just go, Matt. Please?' He took a step towards her. '*Please*,' she said more firmly. 'I need to think things over.'

Without another word he stalked from the room, his back ramrod straight. He closed the door quietly after letting himself out but still Kelly didn't give in to the tears. She hiccuped a few times, desperately trying to hold the tears back until she was sure he'd really gone.

After five minutes, she rose from the chair and carried the cups back to the kitchen, tipping their contents down the sink.

One tear escaped and quivered on the edge of her eyelashes for a second before landing in the sink. Another one followed its course and Kelly's bottom lip started to tremble. Matt didn't love her. The man she'd accidentally fallen in love with didn't love her back.

The tears started to flow, and once the floodgates were opened there was no stopping them. She walked to her bedroom on legs which felt numb, flicked back the bed covers and collapsed onto her bed, being careful of the baby. Curling up into the foetal position, she allowed the darkness of the room to engulf her as the sobs continued to rack her body.

Kelly avoided Matt for the next few days then realised he was doing the same thing. Rhea tried to get her to talk, but Kelly refused.

'I know there's something wrong,' Rhea stated the following Tuesday morning as Kelly was getting ready to leave for Wangaratta.

'How? Woman's intuition?' Kelly asked with a cheeky smile.

'Ha. I didn't need to use it this time. You and Matt have clearly been avoiding each other at all costs.'

Kelly checked the contents of her medical bag, going through her mental checklist to make sure she had everything.

'I've got an idea. Why don't you stay here and talk to him and take my patients? And I'll go to Wangaratta to do the immunisation clinic.'

'You told me you don't like doing the immunisation clinic.'

'See how much I want you to talk to Matt? I'm willing to sacrifice myself for the sake of true love.' Rhea shrugged. 'Besides, the clinic sisters do most of the work, but a doctor has to be there to check things over if necessary.'

'Just as well the GP practices do it on a rotation, then.'

'Yes. Twice a year is enough for me.'

'And this time I'm more than happy to do it for you.'

'Only because you want to get away from Matt. What happened between you two?'

Kelly sighed and looked pointedly at Rhea. 'You said you weren't going to push me for details any more.'

'I lied.' Rhea shrugged. 'You two are perfect for each

other. You work well together—a case in point is how Lorraine and little Justin have coped so marvellously with the huge upheaval in their lives.'

'I'm glad he's been diagnosed and that it didn't take too long,' Kelly said, hoping to stick to this nice, safe topic. 'Lorraine now has a lot of answers she didn't have before and Justin's receiving the attention and care he needs to help him develop.'

'See. That's what I mean. Matt had the knowledge of the local services and could point Lorraine in the right direction and you had the experience of picking up and diagnosing him early. See—a great team.'

'That's just medicine.' Kelly closed her bag and picked up her coat and keys.

'Well, personally, you love him and he loves you.'

'Sure about that?'

Rhea was taken aback. 'What do you mean? Don't you love my brother?'

Kelly shrugged into her coat and picked up her bag. 'I have to go, Rhea, or I'll be late.'

'Come over for dinner tonight,' Rhea said as she walked with Kelly out to the front of the clinic.

'I'll see how I'm feeling.' Kelly waved to Rhea as she walked out the door and across the road to her car. She saw Matt open his front door and step out. She hurried before he saw her, her heart pounding in her chest.

When she reached the car, she looked in her rear-view mirror and saw him enter the clinic. She sagged with relief and shook her head. How was she supposed to survive the rest of her contract here, constantly trying to avoid Matt?

She pushed the thoughts of her future from her mind while she drove to Wangaratta and attended the immunisation clinic. Since she'd arrived, she hadn't really had time to see a lot of Wangaratta, but from the looks of the town hall, which was where the free clinic was held, it was a beautiful city.

After the clinic was over, she wandered around the shops and bought a new pair of shoes and a handbag. That *definitely* made her feel better. When she passed a baby store, the urge to enter was too strong to resist.

In some way, it made her feel as though the child inside her was more real. She couldn't feel it, she hadn't had an ultrasound yet, but Rhea had scheduled one for Friday.

She reached out and touched a little outfit. It was so cute. Tears came to her eyes as she continued to browse. When she came to the babies' cots, she fell instantly in love with one made of lovely polished timber. It seemed so sturdy, so safe. Just right for her baby.

Giving in to the impulse, she decided to order one. The sales assistant was more than happy to oblige her, and by the time Kelly walked out of the store she'd ordered the cot, high chair, rocking chair and change table, which were all part of a set. As she didn't need them delivered for some months, she didn't give an address, still unsure exactly where she was going to relocate once she left Bright.

Even the rain outside wasn't enough to deter her happiness. Regardless of what happened between herself and Matt, she would always have her baby. Although she'd love to stay here in Bright, with Rhea delivering her baby, Kelly wasn't sure she could bear to see Matt every day—loving him the way she did.

She unlocked her car and climbed in. 'Who are you?' she asked out loud. 'If you love Matt, then why aren't you fighting for him? Accept his proposal!' They both knew the attraction between them was so intense it hurt. Surely that was a good sign? Perhaps Matt already loved her but hadn't figured it out yet.

She stopped at a red traffic light, determined to return to

Bright and fight for the man she loved. 'I'm going to get you, Matthew Bentley, and I'm going to get you good!'

The light turned green and she started to move into the intersection. From the corner of her eye she saw a car coming at her from the right. A scream lodged in her throat just before the car hit hers.

A loud crunching noise.

Intense pain.

Blood, which seemed to be everywhere.

CHAPTER TEN

MATT prowled around his consulting room, trying to figure out what was going on.

He'd seen Kelly this morning, hurrying away quickly so they wouldn't have to see each other. The last six days had been close to a nightmare and it was one he was desperate to wake up from.

There was a knock at his door and Rhea came in. 'All finished?' she asked.

'What? Yes,' he answered quickly, before she had a chance to repeat the question.

'Want to talk about it?'

'No, as I've already told you.'

'You know, you and Kelly are as stubborn as each other. I feel sorry for your children.'

'Yeah, they'll have no hope.' He commented without thinking and Rhea crowed with triumph.

'Aha! So you *do* want to have children with Kelly.'

Matt dropped into his chair and slumped forward onto the table. 'I don't know anything any more.'

'It's time to talk, Matt. I've left you long enough, and when Kelly gets back tonight, I'm going to give her an earful as well. You two belong together. Why can't either of you see that?'

Matt raised his head. 'You enjoy playing matchmaker, don't you?'

'Actually...' Rhea preened '...I think I'm quite good. Now, tell me what happened the other night, because one minute I interrupt the two of you kissing in her consulting room and the next minute you're both avoiding each other.'

'Freddy asked her to remarry him.'

'So?'

'Well, she *can't*.'

'Why not?'

'Because I want her to marry me.'

'Why?'

'You sound just like Kelly.'

'Tell me why,' Rhea persisted.

'Because I love her, dammit!' Matt thumped his fist on the desk. 'She belongs with *me*, not with that stuck-up, pretty-boy ex-husband of hers.'

'And have you told her that?'

Matt stopped and thought back. 'Well, kind of. I told her she couldn't marry him.'

'Did you give a reason?'

Matt leaned back in his chair and closed his eyes. 'No.'

'Why not?'

'Because I didn't realise I was in love with her until just now.'

'Gee, you're thick, Matt. Half the town knows you're in love with her. I knew it ten seconds after you met her. You were frowning so hard at her, all dressed in black leathers on that motorbike.' Rhea chuckled. 'She got under your skin. You can tell yourself she's all wrong for you until you're blue in the face, Matt, but the truth is, she's perfect for you. She's nothing like Jana or Louise.'

'No, but she has the ability to hurt me far worse than either of them.'

'She also has the ability to make you ecstatically happy. With the others you had to keep your love of medicine locked away, but with Kelly—you can share it.'

'I know.' He smiled up at his sister. 'Thanks.'

'Hey, that's what I'm here for, honey.'

The phone on his desk rang and he picked it up. 'Dr Bentley. Oh, hi, Natasha. How are things go—?' He stopped speaking and stared at Rhea. 'When?' His voice was deathly quiet. 'I'll be right there.' He slammed the phone down. 'Kelly's had a car accident. She's in A and E right now, having X-rays.'

'What?' Rhea stared at him with her mouth wide open while Matt rushed around the room, trying to find his keys and wondering why his fingers suddenly seemed to be uncooperative.

'You drive carefully,' Rhea said as she came back to reality and followed him out of the room. 'Wait. Pack a change of clothes. Chances are you'll need to stay the night. And take some clothes for Kelly as well.'

'Good idea. Pack a bag for her and meet me at my car in five minutes.' Matt stormed over to his house, wanting nothing than to drive to Wangaratta like a madman. He packed in a hurry, mentally going through what he would need. Toothbrush, shaver, underwear. He ran to his car and waited impatiently for Rhea. The rain was just starting to fall.

'Ring me. Tell me everything as soon as you can, do you hear me?'

'Yes.' He turned and give his sister a kiss. 'I'll bring her back. I'm going to marry her and live happily ever after, and no one is going to stop me.'

'That's the spirit. You just drive safely, Matthew.'

'I will. Kelly needs me.'

'Natasha!' Matt found his friend the instant he stormed into Wangaratta hospital's A and E department. He grabbed her by the shoulders. 'Where is she?'

'She's in Theatre. Matt…' Natasha took his hands from her shoulders. 'Come with me.' She turned to one of her colleagues. 'I'm going on a break now.' Matt allowed himself to be led into a small room with a desk, chair and a stack of hospital case-notes. Natasha closed the door. 'We can talk in here. Have a seat.'

'What's wrong? What's happened?' He couldn't believe how uncertain, how uncomfortable he felt. Kelly was having surgery right this very minute. 'What are her injuries?'

'Matt—' Natasha began.

'The…the baby? What about the baby?'

Natasha shook her head. 'I wasn't sure if you knew she was pregnant. She lost the baby, Matt.'

Matt felt tears sting his eyes as he stared blankly at the wall. He was at a complete loss for words.

'I'm really sorry.' Natasha waited. 'Are you ready to hear this or would you like something to drink first?'

Matt took a deep breath and nodded. 'I'm ready.'

'The car that hit her was travelling at almost eighty kilometres an hour. The driver was thrown from the car on impact and was killed instantly. Kelly's been a lot luckier. She's alive, Matt, and that's what you need to focus on.'

Natasha picked up a piece of paper and read from it. 'She's sustained the following fractures—right scapula, right humerus, right radius and ulna.'

'In other words, her right arm and shoulder are completely smashed up,' he interjected quietly.

'Yes. Right third, fourth and fifth ribs; right femur and a fractured pelvis. Third, fourth and fifth metacarpals are badly crushed as well. She has a seat-belt bruise, but thank God she was wearing it. She also has mild concussion and whiplash. She sustained a bladder rupture and lost the baby, as I've previously said.' She let the piece of paper fall back to the desk.

'She'll make it,' he said forcefully. 'She has to.' Matt looked up at his friend. Her dark auburn hair was pulled back into a bun. It made him realise how much he loved Kelly's bouncy, unruly curls. Natasha's eyes were also green but not as vivid or as happy as Kelly's. 'I need her.'

He clenched his jaw together but his gaze didn't waver. 'I love her.'

Natasha nodded. 'I thought as much.'

'Did she regain consciousness at all?'

'Yes.'

'Does she know about the baby?'

'Yes. She was asking for you, Matt. I stayed with her until she was anaesthetised, and just before she went under she told me how much she loved you.'

Kelly loved him! Surprise was the first emotion to fill his heart before it was replaced with an enormous sense of pride. Kelly loved him. If that was the case, he felt he could cope with anything, even the months of convalescence which were before them.

'I take it by the astonished look on your face you didn't know that?'

Matt smiled goofily up at his friend and shook his head.

'Ah, you're not at *that* stage yet.'

'What stage?'

'The stage where you throw every reservation, every caution to the wind and declare yourselves.'

'No, but we will be as soon as she gets out of Theatre.'

'Maybe…um…wait a few days. This will be pretty hard for Kelly to cope with, Matt—especially losing the baby.'

'But I can help her through it.'

Natasha smiled sadly. 'There are parts you'll never be able to help her through because you'll never know how it felt. She was in the car for two hours with the rain pouring down while they cut her out.'

Matt's jaw clenched again.

'She's lost her baby. She may be in love with you, Matt, but her whole life has been altered by this accident. Physical recovery is just one part of the equation. We know about the endometriosis. She told us and, believe me, grieving takes years to come to terms with. Maybe never.'

Matt noticed tears had welled in Natasha's eyes and he stood up and embraced her for a second. 'Conrad was a good man.'

She edged away and he let her go. 'He *was* a good man, Matt. You're right. He also knew I never loved him the way you and Kelly love each other.'

'What?'

'He knew he was second best.'

'Your first husband.' Matt nodded, watching Natasha impatiently brushing away the tears.

'Be there for Kelly. Just love her, Matt, and regardless of how long it takes or how frustrated you feel, just be there.'

'I will.' He lifted his chin and straightened his shoulders with determination. 'I'm never letting her go.'

'Good.' Natasha opened the door. 'I'd better get back to work.'

'Sure. I need to call Rhea.' As they walked back to the department, Matt took her hand. 'Thanks, mate. You're a good friend.'

'Likewise.' She smiled at him before heading into one of the treatment rooms.

Matt called Rhea and gave her an update. 'I want to stay until she's off the critical list,' he told her.

'No problem. I'll organise a locum tomorrow.'

'Will you be able to cope? I mean, it's not as though there's only one doctor missing—there are two.'

'I'll manage. You just concentrate on Kelly and keep me informed.'

'I will.' Matt hung up and started organising a room at a nearby hotel. He needed to be clear and calm about things. Kelly needed him. She *had* to need him. Didn't she?

'Everything's going to be fine, sweetheart.'

Kelly could hear Matt's voice but she couldn't see him. She wiggled the fingers on her left hand and felt his tighten around hers. Was he really here? Was she dreaming? She'd had the most horrible dream and it didn't help that she ached all over.

She tried to say something, to open her mouth, but it wouldn't work. Next she tried to open her eyes, but even the thought gave her a headache. Tiredness swamped her again and she gave up in favour of sleeping some more.

She drifted in and out of consciousness for a while and every time she could hear Matt's voice either talking to one of the nurses or just talking softly to her, telling her about the wonderful life they were going to have together.

It was a nice thought, a comforting one, as his deep tones surrounded her, making her feel safe and needed before she drifted off to dream of their future together.

The next time she woke, she felt as though she'd been hit by a truck—and then it came flooding back. It hadn't been a truck. It had been a car—a car going through a red light. She listened to the noises around her—the faint beeping of monitors, the sound of soft-soled shoes on the floor, phones ringing—and knew immediately where she was.

She tried to open her eyes. They felt as though they weighed a ton. She persisted and soon could see blurred lights. Waiting for her focus to kick in, she finally realised she was looking at a long pulley which seemed to be suspended above her. Her mind clicked into gear and she realised she must be in traction. How much damage had that car done?

She slowly turned her head, the stabbing pains making her wince.

'Kelly?'

She continued turning her head and sighed with relief when her gaze came to rest on Matt. He'd been sitting in a chair, reading, but now he was standing by her bed so she could see him more clearly.

He reached out a hand and tenderly touched her face. 'Hi, sweetheart.'

'Wh—?' Her throat was dry but Matt came to the rescue, putting a straw between her lips so she could take a sip of water. 'Thanks,' she whispered. 'What time is it?' Her voice was raspy and as she said the words and her head pounded. She closed her eyes again.

'It's almost dinnertime. Are you hungry? I could get some sandwiches for you.'

'No.' The thought of food made her feel instantly sick. She swallowed again and tried to move her arm, only to find she couldn't. She tried the other one and was glad that that one seemed to be working. 'Status?'

Matt chuckled and when she frowned he elaborated. 'You've asked me that question each time you've regained consciousness over the past three days.'

'Three days!' Kelly couldn't contain her astonishment and as her vocal cords were still a little dry she started coughing. Matt quickly held the water out to her and she took another sip. She coughed a little again.

'OK now?' When she nodded, he sat back down, bringing his chair a bit closer. 'You don't remember?'

She shook her head and took another sip of the water. 'Three days?'

'It's been three days since your accident, yes.' His voice was quiet and filled with concern. 'Do you remember much about it?'

Kelly closed her eyes and the memories came flooding back. Tears squeezed out between her closed lashes and she nodded carefully. 'I—I was trapped.' The words were a broken whisper. She opened her eyes and gazed up at Matt, tears falling onto her cheeks, her lower lip trembling. 'Oh, Matt.'

'Honey, honey.' Matt's heart was gripped with pure anguish as he gathered her as close to him as he could. 'Everything's going to be all right, honey. I promise.' He stroked her hair and murmured soothing words as she gently sobbed into his shoulder.

When the tears had finally subsided, he reached for a tissue and wiped her eyes. He held out another tissue and she blew her nose. He took her hand in his again and held it tight, gazing into her red-rimmed eyes.

She looked exhausted and although he knew she needed to rest, especially after that crying session, he couldn't wait any longer. Now was the time.

'Kelly, honey…I know you want to rest and you can. I'm not going anywhere but there's something I have to tell you first.'

Kelly worked hard to keep her eyes open but found she couldn't. She gave a small nod and squeezed his hand, urging him to continue.

'Kelly—I love you.'

Her eyelids opened in surprise and she stared at him for a moment. It was there. She could see it as plain as day. Matt loved her. This wasn't a dream. Her eyes closed again and she sighed, bringing their entwined hands up to her face. She pressed a kiss to the back of his hand and, holding it firmly against her cheek, started to slip into the most wonderful place. A place where she and Matt were dancing, nice and close, loving the feel of being in each other's arms. Both content with their worlds.

'I love you,' she murmured, and he brushed a feathery light kiss across her lips.

This was it. *This* was happiness. She'd found it at last.

The next time Kelly woke, the sun was streaming through the curtains. She frowned for a moment. Had the room changed or had she just imagined it?

'Good morning, beautiful,' Matt's chirpy voice said from beside her. Kelly tried to turn her head but groaned in pain.

'You have minor whiplash,' he told her as he brought his chair around so he was facing her. He stood and pressed a kiss to her lips. 'How's the woman of my dreams feeling this morning?'

Kelly smiled at him. 'Horrible, but better for having seen you.'

'You charmer,' he whispered against her lips, and kissed her once more. 'Glad to see your lips didn't sustain any injuries.'

'It's about the only part of me which feels as though it didn't,' she jested, and then grimaced again as pain shot through her. 'I don't think I'll move at all.'

'Couldn't if you tried, honey. You're so strung up with traction ropes, you've got no hope.'

'You're certainly chipper today,' she accused. 'Stop it.'

Matt laughed, the rich, deep sound filling the small private room. 'I will not and I won't even apologise for feeling wonderful.'

'Why? Because I'm your captive audience?'

'No, that's just an added bonus. Now, let's see, the woman I love is awake—not that she's not incredibly beautiful when she's sleeping.' He ticked the points off on his fingers. 'She's been moved from the critical care unit to a private room—a definite plus as far as spending time with her alone goes. *And* she loves me back. Why *wouldn't* I be chipper?'

Kelly frowned. 'I love you back, eh? Where did you hear that piece of gossip?'

Matt shook his head. 'I've had the added advantage of being with you for the last four days while you've been delirious.'

'That doesn't count.'

'Ahh…I see. Do you remember me telling you last night that I loved you?'

'Yes.'

'And do you remember telling me that you loved me as well, right before you drifted off to sleep?'

Her frown increased. 'Did I?' She'd definitely dreamt it. Had she said the words out loud?

'You most certainly did, but just in case you're going to say that it doesn't count, you can tell me now.'

'Tell you what?'

'Tell me that you love me.'

'Why would I do that?'

He leaned closer. 'Because it's true,' he whispered, a sexy smile on his face. 'I love you and you love me. I dare you to deny it.'

'I double-dare you to prove it,' she pushed, and sighed with longing when he pressed his mouth gently to her own. Kelly brought her free hand up to his head, loving the feel of his hair running through her fingers. The kiss was tender and loving as well as very possessive.

Matt pulled back a fraction. 'Going to deny it?'

'No.' She held his gaze. 'I do love you, Matt.'

'So why deny it just now?'

'And give up those fantastic kisses?' She smiled at him.

'Honey, you don't have to. They're yours and only yours for the rest of your life.'

'What? You don't want to share any with the baby?'

Matt looked surprised and then cautious.

'What is it?' she asked, starting to get worried. A look of pain had entered his eyes and Kelly felt a prickle of apprehension wash over her. 'Matt?'

'You lost the baby, honey. Don't you remember?'

'No. No.' Kelly frowned and dropped her hand from his head. 'No.' She placed it protectively across the blankets on top of her stomach. 'It's still in there.' Her eyes filled with tears. 'It has to be.' The words were whispered out between her trembling lips.

'It's not, honey.' Matt reached for her but she shrugged

away. Pain shot through him at her refusal. 'It's devastating news, Kelly, but we still have each other.' Matt shook his head and watched the tears trickle down her beautiful face. 'You could have died as well, Kelly, but you didn't. We've been given a second chance, honey. I love you. I want to be with you for ever.' He raked a hand through his hair, recalling how wonderful it had felt to have her own fingers doing the same thing only moments ago. 'We're so perfect for each other. We *belong* together.'

'My baby is gone,' she whispered.

'I know, honey, I know, but we'll get through this together.' He reached for her again but once more she shrugged away.

'I want to be alone,' she said, the tears still pouring down her face. Matt wasn't sure that was a good idea, but when Kelly's imploring gaze met his he knew he couldn't refuse.

'Sure. I'll go for a walk and see you in about half an hour.'

'Thanks.'

He leant over and kissed her, glad she didn't pull away this time. He walked to the door, stopping on his way out to look over his shoulder. 'I love you, Kelly. Remember that.'

When he'd gone, Kelly closed her eyes and allowed the tears to fall. Her baby was gone. Gone for ever. She wasn't sure how long she cried for and the emptiness inside seemed to engulf her completely. She was in traction with all sorts of broken bones and an empty womb. Her miracle, the one true miracle in her life, was gone—and she knew there would never be another one.

The knock on the door was barely audible, and as the door started to open Kelly tried to pull herself together, not wanting Matt to see her like this. Had it been half an hour already?

'Hi, there.'

'Natasha.'

'I have a whole ten-minute break so I thought—' Natasha stopped and, seeing the tears that were streaming down Kelly's face, rushed to her side.

'What's wrong? Are you in pain?' She moved the box of tissues onto the bed beside Kelly, who thankfully took one.

Kelly's bottom lip quivered. 'My baby's gone.' She sniffed and blew her nose before Natasha hugged her.

'I know' was all she said. Natasha simply held her, letting her cry her emotions out.

'I feel so…empty. So…lost.'

'I know,' Natasha said again, and Kelly realised she really meant it. Then she remembered Natasha had been widowed twice and although she hadn't lost her child, she'd still lost two husbands.

'I don't want to see Matt just now. I need some—'

'Time,' Natasha finished for her. 'I know. I'll take care of it.'

'He said he'd be back in half an hour but I don't know when he left and—'

'I'll take care of it,' Natasha repeated. She checked her watch. 'My break's over. I'll come back at lunchtime to check on you. Why don't you try sleeping?'

'Hmm. Thanks.'

'That's what friends are for.' Natasha smiled before heading out the door. Her words stayed with Kelly and even though she hardly knew Natasha Forest, she also knew they *would* be friends. Rhea was her friend, and Matt? Matt was definitely her friend, as well as the man she loved.

She bit her bottom lip. Matt loved her and he'd said they would be together, but that seemed so impossible now. She would never be able to give him the family she knew he yearned for. At least, when she'd been pregnant, even though the child hadn't been his, they still could have loved the baby as mother and father.

Now, though, she had nothing to offer Matt. The chance of her getting pregnant again were basically zero. She couldn't do that to him! She couldn't do that to him. She loved him far too much. Besides, she'd fractured her pelvis—that couldn't possibly help her cause. Endometriosis *and* a fractured pelvis. Not much at all to offer the man she loved. He deserved better.

Kelly drifted off into a restless sleep and when she woke up it was dark outside. She slowly craned her neck to the side only to find the chair vacant. Matt was gone.

'It's been three weeks!' Matt stormed as he paced around the hotel room. He was furious.

'Hey, don't shoot me,' Natasha replied. 'I'm just the messenger.'

'How was she today? What did the physio say?'

'The physio is extremely impressed with her. Her surgeons are impressed with her. She's a model patient so the nurses are impressed with her.'

'Everyone's impressed—except me!' he thundered. 'And I'm the man who wants to spend the rest of my life with her.'

'I know,' Natasha said.

'Will you stop staying "I know" and tell me what I'm supposed to do?'

'First of all, Matt, you might try sitting down. I don't think the owners of the hotel will appreciate having to replace the carpet because you've certainly worn a path in it pacing around.'

'That's all I seem to do,' he agreed, but didn't stop. 'What else am I supposed to do? Kelly has refused to see me for three weeks. *Three weeks,* Natasha. At first I listened to you—leave her alone, you suggested. Give her some room. I've done that.'

'I kn—' Natasha stopped when he glared at her. 'Sorry,

she said. She glanced at her watch. 'I have to go home. I want to see Lily before she goes to school this morning.'

'Where is she?' It was the first question he realised he hadn't bellowed since Natasha had walked through his door fifteen minutes ago.

'She's at my neighbour's house. She stays there after school or when I'm on nights.' She shrugged. 'It's convenient.' She walked over and gave him a quick hug. 'Just hang in there. It won't be too much longer.'

'I don't think I can take much more.' He shook his head. 'I can just imagine her beating herself up emotionally, thinking the accident was her fault, thinking losing the baby was her fault—but it wasn't.'

'There's more to it than that, Matt.'

'The fractured pelvis?'

Natasha nodded.

'I've spoken to her specialist. He said there's no reason why she shouldn't be able to carry a baby to full term once her pelvis is completely healed.'

'That's not all, though.'

Matt put his hand to his head and smacked himself. 'The endometriosis.'

'That's right.'

'She thinks she won't fall pregnant again, doesn't she?' Natasha's nod confirmed his suspicions. 'She thinks she can't marry me because she won't be able to give me children, doesn't she?'

Natasha nodded again.

'Fair dinkum, she's the most stubborn woman I've ever met.' Matt reached for the key to his room and started towards the door.

'Do you think this is a good idea?'

'It's the only thing that comes to mind. I've been waiting for the past three weeks for a word that she wants to see me again. I've given her time, Natasha, but I can't wait any

more. I've been torn between being in Bright and working
all hours before rushing back here in case she needed me
I need more stability in my life. *I* need to know that Kell·
is going to be *in* my life. I know she loves me and sh
knows I love her, but that's been about the extent of ou
declarations.'

He shrugged into his coat and reached inside the pocket
pulling out a jeweller's box. 'I've had this burning a hol·
in my pocket for the past two and a half weeks. I want t·
propose to her. I want to know she'll be my wife, and if i
turns out that we can't have any children, then we'll figur·
it out as we go.'

'Matt—'

'Don't try and stop me.' He pulled open the hotel door
'Sometimes a man's gotta do what a man's gotta do!'

'I would never try to stop a man with that sort of gusto.
Natasha laughed. 'Go to it and I'll see you tomorrow.'

Later that day, Matt drove carefully through the rain to th·
hospital and walked down the corridor towards Kelly'
room. Was this the right thing to do? Was he pushing her·
Three weeks he'd waited. Every day he'd held his breath
for some sort of signal from Kelly saying that she was des
perate to see him…but nothing.

He'd hardly slept. He'd hardly eaten anything, and wa:
sure he was well on his way to getting an ulcer from wor
rying about her. She was the first thought he had when h·
woke up and the last when he went to sleep. His dream
had initially been filled with happiness in their promised lif·
together but lately they'd been more about him wandering
around in a wilderness, trying to cut his way through th·
jungle that surrounded him.

He paused momentarily outside her door, determined t·
let her see he loved her—regardless. They belonged to
gether. He hadn't checked with the ward sister as the las

time he'd done that he'd been told Kelly had wanted privacy. Thankfully, most of the nurses were doing their evening after-dinner rounds of their patients.

It was now or never—and never was a prospect he wasn't
willing to entertain. Taking a deep, determined breath, he
turned the handle and opened the door.

A nurse was with her but he purposely stepped through
the door, closing it quietly behind him.

'Dr Bentley!' The nurse was startled but quickly recov-
ered herself. Kelly turned to look at him and he was glad
to note the smooth way her head was now turning. He
couldn't take his eyes off her. She looked…incredible. She
might be in Hamilton-Russell traction, her arm in a plaster
cast and her leg in a splint, but she'd never looked better.
He was mildly conscious of the nurse giving Kelly's sheets
a final tug into place before excusing herself, leaving them
alone.

'Matt.' Kelly stared at him as he slowly advanced towards
her bed. 'I…' She had no idea what to say. What *did* a
woman say to the man she loved, especially when she'd
been putting off seeing him for three weeks?

'You're beautiful,' he stated, coming around the bed so
he was on her left-hand side. He took her hand in his and
raised it to his lips, brushing them lightly across her
knuckles.

Tears welled in her eyes at the gesture. 'I've missed you.'
The words were choked and she started to cry. Matt couldn't
stand being physically apart from her any longer and gathered her close to him—as close as the traction allowed. He
kissed her eyes, her cheeks, her nose, her lips—anywhere
he could.

'Don't ever send me away like that again,' he growled in
her ear as she clung to him. She sniffed a few times and he
tried to pull back to make sure she was really all right, but
the grip of her arm around his neck was strong.

'I love you, Matt,' she whispered, and kissed him. 'I love you so much that I…I have to let you go.'

'Really?' He kissed her back. 'Why is that?'

She let go of him then and turned her face away as though she couldn't bear the shame of what she was about to say. 'Because…because…' Kelly shook her head. 'Because I can't give you children,' she blurted. 'And I know how much you want them.'

Matt breathed out with relief. There. It was out. Out in the open. 'You love me so much you're letting me go? Pushing me into the arms of some other woman—' her head snapped around to meet his gaze '—just so I can procreate? Do you think that would make me happy?' He said the words calmly and clearly, knowing he'd get her attention. 'Come on, Kelly. Surely you know me better than that.'

'I know you want children.'

'I do.' He leaned closer and kissed the tip of her nose. 'But I want *you* more.'

Kelly almost melted. He was so adorable, she'd almost forgotten just how handsome he was. His compelling blue gaze was creating havoc with her heart-rate, her palms were sweaty and her mouth was dry.

'I love you, Kelly. *You.* All of you. And I need all of you, too.'

'But I've been there, Matt,' she protested.

'Where?'

'In a marriage where not being able to conceive was an issue.'

'Yes, but you also told me your ex-husband had a low sperm count. I don't.'

'How do you know?'

'I had a test done this morning.'

'What?' Kelly was amazed. 'How did you get the results this quickly? Oh, no, let me guess—you went to school with the pathologist!'

He laughed. 'That's my girl.'

'Why did you get the test done?'

'To show you how much I love you. We have the opportunity of a long and happy life together. Children would be an added bonus.'

'See, you *do* want children,' she pointed out.

'Yes, and so do you, but what's more important is that I want to have children with *you*. Adoption is an option but so is IVF. Don't let the endometriosis win. You've become pregnant once already—that's an extremely positive sign.'

'Matt, I—'

'Kelly…' He placed a finger over her lips, silencing her. He shrugged out of his thick winter coat before reaching inside his jacket pocket. Kelly held her breath and was surprised when he pulled out a black marker pen.

He walked around the bed to her right side and took off the cap. 'Mind if I sign your cast?' he asked. Before she could reply, he started writing. He shifted his body so he was blocking the view of whatever he was printing, and when he finally moved, Kelly's jaw dropped open.

He'd drawn a big heart with their initials inside. That made her smile. Little hearts were all around the words every woman wanted to read. WILL YOU MARRY ME?

'I know you've probably seen something like this before. After all, you've already been married. But…' He broke off, frowning at her. 'Why are you shaking your head?'

'I've never seen *anything* like this before.' She gazed up at him, her eyes alight with love.

'I was going to bring you flowers but I had no idea what kind you like.'

'I don't,' she told him. 'I prefer plants.'

He shook his head. 'There's still so much I don't know about you.'

'Well, we've got the rest of our lives to find out.'

'Is that a yes?' he asked.

'What's your professional opinion?' she countered.

'That if I *don't* marry you and do it soon, I'll be grey before my next birthday! I need you, Kelly. I need you so much. The past three weeks have been sheer torture.'

'I know. I'm sorry, Matt, but I was so scared.'

'Honey.' He leaned over and kissed her softly. 'We belong together. We can help each other so neither of us are scared ever again.'

'You were scared?'

'Yes. Scared I wasn't going to be able to get through to you.' Matt reached inside his jacket pocket again and pulled out a jeweller's box. When he opened it, Kelly gasped. 'It was my grandmother's.'

She looked at the emerald, encircled with diamonds and couldn't believe how perfect it was. If she'd had to choose an engagement ring out of every ring in the world, she couldn't have chosen better herself. The fact that it was a family heirloom only added to its perfection.

'The emerald is the exact same colour as your eyes,' he whispered, gazing at her. 'Eyes which make me burn with desire and love every time I look into them.' He took the ring from the box and hovered the ring near the third finger on her left hand.

'Well, aren't you going to put it on?' she asked impatiently when he didn't move.

'You haven't given me your answer yet.'

Kelly looked contrite for a moment but quickly smiled. 'Oops.' She looked into his eyes, knowing she had never been happier than right now, this very second. 'Matt, I love you with all my heart. The only answer I *can* give is— Oh, wait a minute. Give me your marker pen.'

Matt did as she asked, thinking she'd write the answer on her cast. Instead, she took his hand in hers and wrote her answer on the back of his hand. He smiled when he read the word, the word which made him the happiest man in the world.

It read…YES.

EPILOGUE

'ONE last push,' Rhea instructed. 'Come on, Kelly, you can do it.'

'That's it, honey,' Matt whispered near her ear, not caring that his hand, which was gripped firmly in hers, had lost all circulation.

Kelly pushed and then finally relaxed, completely exhausted.

'Well done!' Rhea praised, and handed the baby to Kelly.

'It's a girl!' Matt crowed, and kissed first his wife and then his daughter.

'I'm an aunty,' Rhea said proudly, as she set about getting ready to clamp and cut the cord.

'We're grandparents,' said Kelly's parents, who had flown to Australia for the big event. She watched as her parents hugged each other, still as much in love as they'd ever been.

'So are we,' remarked Matt's parents, and she noted a few tears escape her mother-in-law's eyes.

Kelly had wanted a home birth and loved having the people she cared for most with her to witness the miraculous arrival of their baby. Besides, with five doctors and one nurse in the room, she knew she and the baby would be well looked after.

Matt lay down on the bed beside Kelly and kissed her again, tasting her salty tears. 'I'm a dad,' he said proudly.

'And I'm a mum,' she whispered. Tears blurred Kelly's vision as she whispered the words she'd thought she'd

never, ever say. Her life with Matt had been all she'd ever
dreamt about and more, and with the arrival of their daughter, Lisa Jane Bentley, her life had just been enriched a
whole lot more.

LIVE THE EMOTION

Modern Romance™
...seduction and
passion guaranteed

Tender Romance™
...love affairs that
last a lifetime

Medical Romance™
...medical drama
on the pulse

Historical Romance™
...rich, vivid and
passionate

Sensual Romance™
...sassy, sexy and
seductive

Blaze Romance™
...the temperature's
rising

27 new titles every month.

Live the emotion

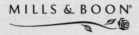

MILLS & BOON®

MB3

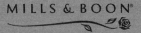

MILLS & BOON

dark angel
LYNNE GRAHAM

Knight in shining armour
or avenging angel?

Available from 21st March 2003

Available at most branches of WH Smith,
Tesco, Martins, Borders, Eason, Sainsbury's
and all good paperback bookshops.

FREE
2 BOOKS
AND A SURPRISE GIFT!

We would like to take this opportunity to thank you for reading this Mills & Boon® book by offering you the chance to take TWO more specially selected titles from the Medical Romance™ series absolutely FREE! We're also making this offer to introduce you to the benefits of the Reader Service™ —

- ★ FREE home delivery
- ★ FREE monthly Newsletter
- ★ FREE gifts and competitions
- ★ Exclusive Reader Service discount
- ★ Books available before they're in the shops

Accepting these FREE books and gift places you under no obligation to buy; you may cancel at any time, even after receiving your free shipment. Simply complete your details below and return the entire page to the address below. *You don't even need a stamp!*

YES! Please send me 2 free Medical Romance books and a surprise gift. I understand that unless you hear from me, I will receive 4 superb new titles every month for just £2.60 each, postage and packing free. I am under no obligation to purchase any books and may cancel my subscription at any time. The free books and gift will be mine to keep in any case.

M3ZEC

Ms/Mrs/Miss/Mr ....Initials ....
BLOCK CAPITALS PLEASE

Surname ....

Address ....

....

....Postcode ....

Send this whole page to:
UK: FREEPOST CN81, Croydon, CR9 3WZ
EIRE: PO Box 4546, Kilcock, County Kildare (stamp required)

Offer valid in UK and Eire only and not available to current Reader Service subscribers to this series. We reserve the right to refuse an application and applicants must be aged 18 years or over. Only one application per household. Terms and prices subject to change without notice. Offer expires 30th June 2003. As a result of this application, you may receive offers from Harlequin Mills & Boon and other carefully selected companies. If you would prefer not to share in this opportunity please write to The Data Manager at the address above.

Mills & Boon® is a registered trademark owned by Harlequin Mills & Boon Limited.
Medical Romance™ is being used as a trademark.